WHEN WINC...
PEOPLE LISTEN

Shop Our Other Locations

His unknown enemy behind the cottonwood seemed intent on gunning him with that long-nosed Remington Dragoon. So it would have been safer to shoot first and ask questions later. Longarm trained his Winchester on the cuss from close behind and called out, "Freeze in your place and let that horse pistol fall wherever it has a mind to."

The man let go of the Remington as Longarm's tensed-up senses picked up the soft metallic snick of some other gun's safety.

So Longarm wasn't there anymore as a shotgun blast opened a black slab of shadow behind him. For he'd spun into the street and fired as the sneak with the scattergun put a full double load of number-nine buck into his pal against the cottonwood, then stepped out into better light to drop his smoking ten-gauge and belly flop down atop it, as anyone else might have with a round of .44-40 so close to his shock-frozen heart. . . .

*   *   *

SPECIAL PREVIEW!

Turn to the back of this book for an exciting excerpt from the blazing new series . . .

Desperado

DON'T MISS THESE
ALL-ACTION WESTERN SERIES
FROM THE BERKLEY PUBLISHING GROUP

THE GUNSMITH by J. R. Roberts

Clint Adams was a legend among lawmen, outlaws, and ladies. They called him . . . the Gunsmith.

LONGARM by Tabor Evans

The popular long-running series about U.S. Deputy Marshal Long—his life, his loves, his fight for justice.

LONE STAR by Wesley Ellis

The blazing adventures of Jessica Starbuck and the martial arts master, Ki. Over eight million copies in print.

SLOCUM by Jake Logan

Today's longest-running action western. John Slocum rides a deadly trail of hot blood and cold steel.

TABOR EVANS

LONGARM

ON THE BUTTERFIELD SPUR

JOVE BOOKS, NEW YORK

LONGARM ON THE BUTTERFIELD SPUR

A Jove Book / published by arrangement with
the author

PRINTING HISTORY
Jove edition / April 1993

ISBN: 0-515-11082-5

Jove Books are published by The Berkley Publishing Group,
200 Madison Avenue, New York, New York 10016.
The name "JOVE" and the "J" logo
are trademarks belonging to Jove Publications, Inc.

PRINTED IN THE UNITED STATES OF AMERICA

10 9 8 7 6 5 4 3 2 1

LONGARM

ON THE
BUTTERFIELD SPUR

Chapter 1

The mad-dog career of Gargoyle Gibson was brought to its end on a grim Friday morning in downtown Denver with the assistance of Rutherford B. Hayes of Ohio.

The nineteenth President of These United States had intended something else entirely when he'd handed down his picky rules on the dress and deportment of federal employees. But the end result that morning, way out West, was Deputy U.S. Marshal Custis Long catching holy hell about his hat when he reported in for court duty at the Denver federal building.

Longarm, as he was better known to friend and foe alike, saw nothing wrong with his old sepia Stetson, its crown telescoped in the High Plains fashion and the few bullet holes in the flat brim barely noticeable. But when he pointed out he'd be sitting there hatless in his sissy three-piece suit of tobacco tweed, he only drew more fire from his boss, Marshal William Vail, who thundered up from his less imposing height, "Judge Dickerson will be expecting you to march the accused in and out at gunpoint, with your *hat*—and let me repeat your *hat*—on! So get your ass over to Seventeenth Street and pick yourself up some decent headgear before the afternoon session. I don't want to talk about it no more."

Longarm figured that likely meant his pudgy but hard-

1

shelled old boss was in no mood to argue. So he just nodded amiably and allowed he'd best get cracking if he aimed to treat himself to a new spring bonnet before lunchtime.

He was braced for Billy Vail to demand he take care of his own violations of the departmental dress code on his own damned time. But the two of them had ridden high and low together long enough to sense how far either ought to push. So Longarm was out of earshot by the time Vail warned him not to spring for anything cheaper than a Stetson brand Carlsbad. But Longarm knew what sort of hat he needed for a job like his that called for such a variety of chores.

He also knew a spanking-new Stetson Carlsbad, shipped all the way from Philadelphia, would surely whittle a week's pay down to the stump. So when he got to the bottom of the stone steps out front, he didn't head for the main shopping district at all. He moseyed up to Broadway and Welton, scowling at his own tall reflection in shop windows as he drifted south, trying to recall just where the hell he'd seen that small hat repair shop that swore they could fix you up with a steam cleaning and reblocking while you waited.

There weren't many gents abroad to ask, at this hour of a weekday. Denver's Broadway ran along the apron of Capitol Hill, where the business district commenced to give way to housing, both boarding and private, becoming downright fancy as one worked up the slope to what was more the true level of the High Plains than a real hill.

Downtown Denver had mushroomed on the lower flood plains of a muddy river called the South Platte, where it was joined by the smaller flow and gold-bearing sands of Cherry Creek. Folks who'd panned that gold, or the pockets of those who had, liked to live on somewhat higher ground.

The big flood of '64 had inspired heaps of fancy homes along the tree-shaded avenues up to the east, even as it had offered a grand opportunity to rebuild the business district from scratch.

Longarm spotted a cigar-store Indian he knew, down by Tremont Place, and suddenly found his bearings. He thanked

2

the basswood warrior with a nod and swung the next corner to find that, sure enough, the hole-in-the-wall he was after still stood near that last stage stop in town—assuming they were still running coaches out to the east along that Overland feeder line.

Entering the dingy little shop, Longarm found himself lost in a sweaty felt-scented fog with a balding gnome and a cowboy. He'd have bet money the small brown cuss in the skullcap and a canvas apron knew more about cleaning and blocking hats than anyone in a checked shirt and batwing chaps. So that was who he asked about his hat, which looked to him like it was still worth saving.

The gnomish hatter examined it dubiously, but said, "So maybe, with a little glue sizing, a little dye, and a lot of steam. But I have to take care of this other gentleman's Buckeye first. So would you like to wait or come back already?"

Longarm said he'd as soon wait, as long as it was all right for him to smoke. When the hatter said it was, Longarm produced five cents' worth of three-for-a-nickel cheroots just to be a sport, and lost when the younger customer with the bigger hat took him up on his offer.

The older hatter declined and turned away to check on the fool kid's Buckeye, which was impaled on sycamore inside a copper steam jacket. The cowboy at least had the manners, and matches, to light them both up as they stood closer to the greasy glass door. Longarm knew the glass had been wiped with glycerine soap to keep it from fogging over from the warm humidity inside. He supposed even a gnome liked to glance outside now and again when things were slow.

But it was the young cowboy, facing the glass more directly, who shook out his match with a whistle of pure admiration to say, "Would you look at that and tell me I ain't just died and gone to heaven, pard?"

Longarm turned, lit cheroot gripped between his grinning teeth, to grunt in agreement at the pulchritude of the female figure mounting the high curb across the way, apparently aiming to enter a small German delicatessen store. As she vanished inside with a flurry of her apricot Dolly Varden skirts, the kid who liked big hats and free smokes told Longarm just what he'd like to do to such a fine-figured filly.

Longarm hadn't asked. He sighed and softly replied, "I hope you won't take this less friendly than it's meant, cowboy. But I was brought up to talk a mite more respectful about any lady who's never given me call to disrespect her."

To which the younger man felt obliged to reply, "Aw, hell, a real lady would have had herself a proper escort in this part of town, and couldn't you see she was strutting about in high heels?"

Longarm smiled thinly and murmured, "So are you, now that you tell me that's the way to judge a lady's character a pistol shot away. But I won't call you no whore if you'd like to behave more like a gentleman in the company of folk you just don't know worth spit."

The old hatter cut through the tension he felt in the steamy air of his little shop by calling out, "Before we fight a duel over a lady in high heels, could she by any chance have her brown hair up under a veiled straw boater? Also light muslin skirts ruffled high enough in the back to show pinker petticoat frills?"

Longarm just took a thoughtful drag on his cheroot as the rude youth in batwing chaps allowed that the old hatter had described the object of their considerable admiration to the bone.

The old hatter chuckled and said, "I thought so. Three times a week at about this time of day she picks up enough to feed either a small family or two honeymooners, despite what Eichbaum charges."

"You mean she's already got a swain?" said the cowboy, who'd just volunteered to come on her all three ways at once.

The hatter shrugged and replied, "So who can explain why other men should like boys or even ugly women? Like I said, that one is shopping for at least two. But confidential, I'd rather kiss the asshole of our pussycat at home than such a face as hers!"

Longarm smiled thinly at the picture. He had to allow the kid he'd been correcting had a point, though, when the cowboy insisted, "Oh, shit, ain't no gal ugly as *that,* Pop!"

The old hatter shrugged again. "So kiss her when she comes out if you want. You'll see she's got a harelip. I mean, her face is split up the front so her mouth runs up into her nose, just the way a rabbit's mouth does. When she comes back out you'll see she wears a winter-weight veil on her summer hat. Just between the three of us, it doesn't hide enough!"

As the old hatter turned back to have another look at the Buckeye he was blocking, he added with a knowing sigh, "*Mensh tracht, Gott lacht!* Such a figure and not a bad face, from the nose up."

Longarm's tobacco smoke tasted sour all of a sudden as he saw the gal in the veiled boater and Dolly Varden coming out of the small food shop with a big string bag of food. Enough to last a small family a day, or a couple a bit longer. The old hatter had just said she shopped no more than three times a week, at a time her man, like most men, would be at work, if he had a job.

You couldn't make out her deformation at first, as she toted her grub their way across the nearly deserted cobblestones. The boy in the batwings marveled, "Hell, she looks as good coming as she does going, and ain't June busting out all over under that frilled summer bodice!"

Longarm muttered, "Don't talk dirty about the poor gal. I ain't going to say that again." Then, as she got closer, oblivious to them watching her through the grimy glass, the sunlight hit her face just right, or wrong, and it was the cowboy who gasped, "Aw, shit, Lord, that just wasn't *fair* of you, hear?"

Longarm felt the same pang of sick pity as the hideously split-faced girl of no more than twenty or so swerved to mount the curb on their side at a more merciful angle. Longarm was a decent man who sincerely liked most folks. So his feelings for her misfortune were sincere. But after that he was a lawman. So he had a hand on the door latch as he casually asked the

5

old hatter what they said about the gent that poor ugly gal had to shop for so often at the prices charged across the way.

When the old hatter could only say he'd heard she lived with a sort of squat but well-dressed and kind of quiet man, Longarm was already gliding out the door, ignoring the older man's promise to fix his old Stetson any minute now.

That Dolly Varden outfit was easy to keep track of from a distance as he tailed it catty-corner across the sunny street she was moving west on now. He was glad he was a good ways back when she suddenly stopped near an alley entrance, looked long and hard both ways, and ducked out of sight.

Longarm picked up his own pace, keeping to the far side as he cut the line of that alley entrance without slowing, and managed to spy just a flash of Dolly Varden ruffles whipping through the backyard fence beyond some trash cans, about four backyards down on the right. So, seeing that it seemed safe, he retraced his steps on the far side, and moseyed into that same alley as if he were looking to take a leak, or make sure of some infernal street address.

Once he finished, Longarm moved back out to the street and drifted over to Tremont Place. Sure enough, he spotted a uniformed roundsman of the Denver P.D. holding up a wall with his back, on the shady side, near the stage stop.

The roundsman stared thoughtfully at Longarm, and even let go of the wall to stand straighter as he waited to see what a pesky citizen in a fairly neat suit and really battered hat might want.

Longarm had been hoping to find a copper badge he'd worked with in the past. But since they didn't know one another, he broke out his wallet to flash some identification and his federal badge while mentioning a few names of people he knew on the force.

The roundsman had heard how his own Sergeant Nolan had been promoted after helping the famous Longarm check out a hunch about a moving dray loading up behind the Tabor mansion up on the hill, at a time neither Silver Dollar Tabor nor his Miss Augusta seemed to be home. So he now assured

Longarm he stood ready and able to arrest as many harelipped gals in Dolly Vardens as the peace and quiet on his beat called for.

Longarm held up his hand. "There's no outstanding warrants on the gal, even if she turns out to be the one and original Splitlip Sally."

The copper badge looked so downcast Longarm felt obliged to add, "There's no federal statute against an unfortunate maiden marrying up with an even uglier cuss, as long as we can't prove she'd aided and abetted him at something more serious than mere feeding and fornicating. Under common law, a wife has the right to do that much for a lawful husband, however unlawful the skunk might be."

"Then we're after the harelip's husband?" asked the copper badge.

It seemed about time. Longarm said, "His name's Gaylord Gibson, as only a mother could have sprinkled such a homely child a good twenty-seven years ago. He's better known as Gargoyle Gibson, partly due to his own unfortunate looks and partly because of his odd habit of lurking above the scenes of future crimes drawing maps. He's said to be the boss or the advance scout for the Scarecrow Gang, as some call that ragged-ass band of road agents. Are you with me so far?"

The copper badge, who answered to the handle of Curtis, said he'd read in the *Rocky Mountain News* about that stage-coach job up the other side of Rowena in the Front Ranges. Then he proved he'd been paying attention by pointing at a nearby sign to add, "And Jesus H. Christ! That's the stop for the Overland to Beecher Island on the Arikaree!"

Longarm allowed he'd been wondering if that stage spur still ran that far. Then he warned, "I could still be wrong. The notorious Splitlip Sally can't be the only serious harelip out our way, and there's no law against hiring a furnished room near a stage stop, or even paying too much for cooked meat and cheese instead of just eating out, like everyone else, if you ain't got a proper kitchen."

7

Then he reached under his frock coat for the double-action he packed cross-draw and thumbed an extra round of .44-40 into its cylinder to make it six-in-the-wheel, instead of the safer five a man felt more comfortable about in less trying times. As his newfound sidekick followed suit with a Colt .36 Longarm warned him, "We don't want needless gunplay, even if it's really Gibson, and his ugly but otherwise innocent wife ain't in the line of fire. I don't have to tell you how much explaining we'll have to do if I've just jumped to a sensible but wrong conclusion, do I?"

The copper badge sounded cheerful enough as he replied, "I won't have to explain shit, Longarm. You're the senior officer and I'm just backing your play. So would you like to tell me what the play might be now?"

Longarm chuckled wryly and replied, "The old knock on the front door and a sneakier lawman out back, of course. Like I said, it looks like a rooming house from the back. You'd know better than me why a gal might have to duck out for grub when you can get room and board for less than all this store-bought bullshit adds up to."

The copper badge asked Longarm to repeat the street address. As soon as he did the lawman, who knew the neighborhood a heap better, shook his head and said, "That ain't no rooming house. I didn't know anyone still lived above the cabinetmaker's shop on the ground floor. The Swansons, Magnus Swanson being the owner, moved up on Lincoln Street as soon as their cabinet work started to pay off. Can't say I blame 'em. Have you ever smelled boiling glue on a hot summer's eve? Swanson must have hired them empty quarters to them ugly folks, and I know he wouldn't want anybody cooking food up yonder after closing hours, what with all that veneer, varnish, lacquer, and such locked up on the premises."

Longarm was still thinking as the copper badge went on. "Won't be locked up right now, though. I'm sure they're working in the shop downstairs even as we speak. So why don't we just go ask old Magnus Swanson who he's got up in his old quarters?"

8

Longarm nodded, but kept thinking as the two of them retraced his steps around to where he'd last seen that Dolly Varden outfit acting so peculiar. Longarm had long since learned, in the six or eight years he'd been riding for the Justice Department, how peculiar even innocent folk could act when they thought nobody else was looking. But with every step toward that cabinetmaking shop he felt better about this particular hunch. So as the copper badge pointed to a small swinging sign a few doors down the mixed block of mostly frame house-fronts, and allowed he knew the cabinetmaker on a first-name basis, Longarm decided his initial plan made even more sense now. The copper badge would go in the front way, and Longarm would wait out back.

As they parted near the corner, Longarm repeated his warning about hasty gunplay, explaining, "Lots of old boys act a mite proddy for no sensible reason. So remember Gargoyle Gibson's easy description. He's a tad older than you but some few summers younger than me. After that he's uglier than you, me, and his ugly wife put together. They suspect he's got some bone disorder. Humpback, as well as a face so gnarly that witnesses have described it as a mask. If you meet up with anyone less scary I've likely had mean thoughts about another pathetic couple entirely. Give me two full minutes before you drift in to question the old boy you know."

So that was the way they worked it and it worked like a charm. Longarm had been hunkered behind those trash cans a spell, an unlit cheroot clenched between his bared teeth as he fought the temptation to light it, when he heard leather grating on cinders and hunkered lower. Then that rear gate slowly creaked open and that awful female face was staring his way, but not seeing him. Then it swung to stare the other way.

She must have told the cuss she was scouting for that it was safe to make his next move. For the next move of Gargoyle Gibson involved a crablike scuttle out the gate, a Schofield .45-28 in each gnarled fist.

There was no doubting the identity of such a literally warped character. Longarm wondered, absently, how even an ugly harelip could kiss such a mutt, even in the dark, as he waited for his wanted man to twist the other way in his expensive albeit poorly fitting black suit. Then he drew a deadly bead on the outlaw and called out, not unkindly, "Freeze like a statue or die like a dog long before you can turn around, Gibson!"

Then the fool outlaw's foolish wife tore out that gate, wailing at Longarm not to kill her sweet Gaylord, and Longarm was sure one of the three of them had to wind up dead as she got between him and a desperate asshole with a gun in each hand!

But then Gibson had let both Schofields thud to the cinders to either side of him as he clawed for some sky, shouting, "Don't you hurt my Funny Bunny! She had nothing to do with stopping that Rowena stage!"

Longarm told him to flatten both empty hands against a tall board fence he happened to be facing as, meanwhile, the aptly named Funny Bunny kept coming, blubbering at him not to gun her Huggy Hump.

He fired a round into the gritty dirt between them in a vain attempt to fend her off and attract some damned assistance. The dust and cinders peppering the pleats of her Dolly Varden skirt didn't even slow her down. Longarm had to grab her with his free arm, hard, to swing her out to one side as he kept his .44-40's muzzle aimed at her grotesque husband, cussing the both of them under his breath as she wriggled, wept, and pleaded with a heap of spit, snot, or both running down her exposed front teeth and far more gums than he was really interested in gazing upon.

Her wriggles felt sort of interesting, although he now saw why that old hatter had said he'd rather kiss a cat's asshole. He got her to stop shoving her face in his by threatening to shoot her Huggy Hump if she didn't simmer down. That inspired her not to grind her pelvis into his left hip so hard either. But that was likely just as well. A man had no call to get it up for any gal that inspired such contradictory feelings at either end.

As Longarm had hoped, that one pistol shot soon had his copper-badged sidekick tearing out that same back gate, a

10

club and drawn .36 ready for anything until he saw at a glance that Longarm had one freak against a far fence and the other in his arms. Then the younger lawman marveled, "They slickered me! Them Mex cabinetmakers I was talking to downstairs were telling me that the couple who'd hired the upstairs rooms had just moved out!"

Longarm said, "Pick up them two army pistols near that rascal's feet, will you? We'll talk about mysterious Mexicans in a Swedish shop after we got these two handcuffed and under tighter control."

As the copper badge scooped up his Schofields, Gargoyle Gibson sobbed, "Not her! *Me,* you danged fools! I'm the one as scouted the Rowena stage for the boys. Sweet little Sally didn't know a thing about it!"

Longarm kept the humpback covered as the copper badge cuffed his hands behind his deformed spine. Then Longarm holstered his own six-gun and swung the nicely built harelip the other way as he reached for the federal cuffs on the back of his own gunbelt, muttering, "Like the old song says, farther along we'll know more about it. Meanwhile, on at least two occasions before that Rowena stage was stopped, with the U.S. mail and a mining payroll aboard, an outstandingly funny-looking couple, no offense, rode the stage the length of that feeder line down from Lyons. It wasn't until after the stage crew had been stopped by this gang of scarecrows a mile or so from Trapper's Rock that they recalled the male passenger asking heaps of questions about the surrounding mountain scenery. They tell us one of the road agents dressed up like a scarecrow was sort of humpbacked too. Ain't that a bitch?"

Longarm was cuffing the harelip—it wasn't easy—as her ugly husband insisted, "You just heard me confess in full to robbing your danged old U.S. mails. So why would I lie and say my sweet little Funny Bunny only come along for the ride?"

Having his own prisoner cuffed and under wrigglesome control for the moment, Longarm told the copper badge, "We'd

11

best march 'em over to your nearest precinct house near City Hall, Curtis. Denver P.D. deserves to be included, and I'll send for some help from the federal lockup, down by the depot, while we make sure they spell your name right on the Denver blotter."

The copper badge beamed and said he felt much obliged. Then, as they were marching their prisoners down the alley, he asked, "What if he's telling the truth, Longarm? What if that poor gal there didn't know her husband was up to no good?"

Longarm replied, "That ain't our worry, old son. She'll get her chance to state her case in court. If they decide she was only a total imbecile they'll likely let her go. If they decide she might have known a dapper dresser with no visible means and a taste for delicatessen grub had to be up to something, they likely won't."

The harelip Longarm was leading by one elbow commenced to cry like a little kid being punished for something she hadn't done. A man needed a colder heart than Longarm's if he meant to treat the poor dumb shit professionally. So even though his brain warned him he was being foolish, his fool mouth told the wretched young freak nobody was going to hurt her and that he'd see she got to talk to a smart lawyer from the public defender's office before they booked her on federal charges.

Her misshapen mate, trudging along beside her, said soothingly, "Don't you worry, Funny Bunny. You just keep still and let me take all the blame, like I always promised I would, hear?"

It was hard to understand her answer. She didn't talk so good when she wasn't so upset. Gargoyle Gibson caught Longarm's eye to add, "I ain't gonna let you bastards put her away. She didn't know enough to matter, and even if she had, I purely love my Sally."

Longarm didn't answer. In his six or eight years with the Justice Department he'd learned most anything was possible. And toads made love to other toads in the spring, when you thought about it.

12

Chapter 2

Longarm figured the jails were so crowded with all those smart crooks because the smartest crook couldn't seem to figure out the edge the law started out with.

There were so many lawmen it didn't really matter whether they were half as smart as any self-appointed mastermind of crime who couldn't grasp the odds against him.

It was a lot like thinking one could buck the house at roulette with a month's pay and yet another new system. A casino worthy of the name had the chips to cover every bet until, sooner or later, the poor little shit with a system bet wrong.

Lawmen bet their own numbers instead of chips against poor shits with new systems. Thanks to all the city, state, and other federal lawmen anxious to be cited for assisting in the capture of Gibson's notorious gang, Longarm managed to get his hat steamed and blocked that afternoon after all, while others tidied up all the questions the humpback and his harelipped Sally hadn't answered by the time Longarm saw the last of them at the federal house of detention just in time for some free food and needled beer at the Parthenon Saloon.

By quitting time, Henry, the pasty-faced youth who played on the typewriter in Marshal Vail's front office, had produced carbon copies on onionskin paper for Longarm and the other deputies. So afterward, Longarm had some time to kill as he flirted with the new barmaid in the Black Cat.

He didn't think that particular barmaid put out for customers. Few of them did. But the flirting was more interesting than a lot of self-serving fibs on onionskin paper, and just drinking there till the sun went down would have been really dumb.

He was waiting for the sun to go down because the snooty neighbors of a high-toned young widow woman up on Capitol Hill had been upsetting her with uncouth remarks about a certain gentleman caller who wore ready-made duds and had to work for every dime he had in this world.

It was just as easy to slip in through her kitchen door from the back alley after dark, and it likely saved a lot of tea-tray talk in her front parlor. For as she'd promised, the Junoesque young widow woman had her light brown hair down and wore nothing but her brown brocade kimono and a pair of kick-off slippers as she let him in the back way, with no lamps lit on the ground floor, barred that door behind him, and hauled him upstairs, cussing her own weak nature all the way, to where she'd laid out a swell supper for the two of them in the sort of small drawing room she had built into what she liked to call her bedroom suite.

When folks were rich enough they didn't have to put up with plain and simple bedrooms such as *he* could afford, over on the far less fashionable side of Cherry Creek. This pretty young thing had been left so much dinero by her late mining magnate husband that she even had indoor plumbing just for her sweet self—and any bedroom guests, of course—on the other side of the bedroom.

But she said she wanted to eat first, and Longarm was hungry enough to indulge her in that desire as well. He figured one of the reasons she curved in and out so well, and was so soft, was her healthy appetite for real food. He'd met rich folks who seemed to feel they had to prove it by eating fancy shit they never would have thought of eating if it hadn't been so expensive. But the pleasingly plump gal with her kimono already starting to hang open had prepared a repast of pickled

14

red cabbage, pork chops, and fried potatoes, washed down with coffee strong enough to remove paint before she'd laced it with brandy.

He knew she'd only put the brandy in to sweeten it some. But he wasn't worried about the coffee keeping them awake either. He just dug in, and having been raised in the country, he'd have just chewed and swallowed till he'd cleaned his plate. But seeing as she lived on Capitol Hill and all, she seemed to expect supper guests to carry on a conversation with her across the small rolling table as they supped. So he told her about the day he'd just had.

She seemed to really care whether Splitlip Sally was likely to wind up in prison or not as, meanwhile, she served him cherry pie with tangy cheddar cheese. He told her he doubted they had much of a case against the poor ugly critter, as long as she and her ugly man stood by the same story.

Washing down some pie and cheese, he explained, "Under common law, a spouse can't be forced to testify against a spouse. But that don't prevent a spouse from testifying *for* a spouse. So smart prosecutors try to steer clear of such pickles. Makes no sense to let a jury hear an outlaw's woman swear how kind he can treat his horse if you can't make her hazard a guess as to where he might have ridden the brute the day of the robbery."

She said she still felt sorry for any woman forced to take up with a road agent who looked like a gargoyle, unless that woman didn't want to sleep with just her own hand.

Longarm cocked a friendly brow at her and replied, "You ain't seen the natural disaster the poor gal married up with. I swear I'd sleep with my own hand a lot before I'd go to bed with either of 'em."

He polished off the last of his pie and added with a thoughtful frown, "I've been sort of wondering about that marriage certificate she was packing all the time, though. Denver P.D. said it spoiled any chance they had to nail 'em on a local morals charge. But it sort of sticks in my craw, if only I could figure out why."

She poured him more coffee as she suggested, "Perhaps they were more self-conscious about checking in and out of places than your more, ah, average couple?"

Longarm said, "That's what Billy Vail says. I asked him about him and his own old woman, when they go off to stay at that fancy resort hotel up Leadville way."

The widow woman looked away, eyes blurred by a bittersweet memory she didn't want to go into at the moment with another man as she softly murmured, "I don't think they require their guests to show marriage certificates at the Claredon House."

He nodded. "That's what Billy Vail says. Nobody who's been married more than an army hitch packs a fool marriage certificate around. Yet the Gibsons swear, and their papers prove, the two of 'em got hitched out Utah way, three years ago, when she was seventeen and only answering to Sally Kirby."

The widow frowned and asked if the poor thing had been a Mormon maiden. But Longarm shook his head and explained, "She was a wagon train accident. Born on the way West to folks who took one look at her and left her by the side of the trail, wrapped in a flour sack without so much as a note giving her real name. A kinder cowhand found her, and an elderly couple called Kirby took her in and named her after a kid of their own who'd died of the cholera. She told a friendly matron at the house of detention she thinks them nesters might have been Papists. They never took her to the nearby Mormon temple, and there weren't no other churches out their way."

He finished his cup, considered lighting up, and decided not to as his voluptuous hostess asked if anyone was going to get in touch with the obviously decent old couple about the arrest of an adopted daughter.

He shrugged and said, "She tells us they're both dead. The old man died when she was younger. The old woman sold the spread and they moved in to Ogden. Then *she* died, just before Gargoyle came along to take Sally away from all that. Civil ceremony at the Ogden city hall. We already checked

16

that part by wire. Like I said, it's unusual to worry folks will accuse you of living in sin with a mud fence. But maybe you'd have to marry up with a mud fence to get the point. I'd feel silly but hardly ashamed if anyone accused me of living in sin with anyone pretty as *you*."

She flustered, "I'd have to leave town, you big oaf! In the meanwhile, I'd hardly call these, ah, social visits living with one another any way at all. Would you like an after-supper brandy while I clear the table, darling?"

He allowed there was enough in his coffee already, and offered to help. He figured it was the least he could do, seeing she always gave her servants the whole weekend off when he was there.

She told him he didn't have to, but of course she let him, and he brought her up to date on other odd angles about the Scarecrow Gang as they toted everything down to the kitchen in the dark.

Those Mexicans who'd told Roundsman Curtis they were cabinetmakers employed by Magnus Swanson had sort of faded from view by the time the Gibsons had been booked and someone went back to see what had really been going on.

It now seemed that what had really been going on involved the original owners of the business selling out to another so-called cabinetmaker, who might have been some sort of Latin but hadn't looked like either Gargoyle Gibson or the Mexicans messing about with woodworking tools and glue pots down below. From their cells down by the depot neither Gibson seemed able, or willing, to shed any light on that. Questioned separately, they'd both agreed old Gargoyle had hired the empty rooms upstairs from a landlord who looked a lot like that gray fuzz you find under the beds of a second-rate hotel.

When the widow woman suggested a new owner who'd let space to one shifty tenant would likely let space to another, Longarm said, "That's how Billy Vail and the county clerk see it. As of now there's nobody on the premises, and the new owner can't be found because there's no such name in the county directory."

Then, because by then they'd piled all the dirty dishes in the sink and nobody could see into her dark kitchen from outside, he took her in his arms and added, "I never trudged all the way up this hill to jaw about my day at the office. So prepare to meet a fate worse than death, my proud beauty."

She laughed girlishly and pleaded, "Oh, no, you villain! I am not that kind of girl. Or at least I'm not that kind of a girl on a kitchen table, you big oaf!"

But by then he was moving her from her half-sitting position against the edge of the big pine table to a more spread-eagled position on her back, and that kimono sure draped swell as she spread her big shapely thighs to sigh, "But wearing that silly gunbelt, dear?"

He unbuttoned and unbuckled everything as he entered her with a gasp of pure pleasure, having forgotten how sweet her familiar flesh felt around his first thrusts since he hadn't had her for a while.

It still felt grand as he kept on thrusting, standing upright in his boots as he undressed himself while driving her loco, she said, with his deep but almost casual investigation of her inner being—as she liked to call her old ring-dang-doo.

She said he was teasing hell out of her that way. He said he *wanted* to tease the both of them, to make up for all the lonesome nights since last they'd been this close to one another. But then she shrugged out of her kimono completely, and reached up to haul him down atop her heroic bare breasts as she kicked off her slippers and locked her bare ankles high up his spine, talking dirty as a trail-town whore as he did his best to carry out suggestions that sounded like a heap of fun until one tried them.

After she'd come with her bare tailbone hammering hard pine, she suggested and he agreed they'd be able to do it harder, without permanent injury, on a softer surface. So leaving their duds scattered across the kitchen, Longarm carried her out and off to her front parlor, still impaled on his erection and hanging on for dear life with her arms and legs.

18

He knew why she got such a boot out of screwing naked in the front parlor, where she usually poured tea for visiting society matrons, ministers, and such. For she'd told him as much on the occasion he'd thrown it to her dog-style in her bay window with the street lamp out front casting romantic shadows on her ample bare ass.

But on this occasion he felt more like kissing an old pal. So he did, a lot, as he screwed her deep but not all that fancy aboard the horsehair settee she usually sat on with guests who were far less fun. She didn't mind his kissing her so much when he was pounding her to glory. Decent women seldom did. But after they'd come and paused to breathe for a change, with him still in the saddle, she murmured, "You certainly seem kissy this evening, Custis. Do I remind you of any other lady we know, or just those wicked circus performers in the *Police Gazette*?"

He chuckled, kissed her again less passionately, and told her he liked really naked thighs better than anything he'd ever seen in circus tights. He hadn't been consciously thinking of anybody else in particular, not this early in their screwing. But he knew what she meant. He just didn't understand why women had to spread their inner thoughts like jam all over the magic. Few men were dumb enough to tell the gal they were in bed with about the swell blow job another gal had given them in a hayloft long ago and far away. Everybody old enough to be worth getting horny with had heaps of horny memories about other folks. But who in thunder wanted to know somebody they were fixing to come with was sort of wishing they'd move more like Tom, Dick, or Lorena had that moonlit night down by the willows?

This particular gal, who might have felt even better between her thighs if she'd grown up riding astride, like that good old gal up Montana way he was never going to see alive again, was working herself up for bedtime confessions, he could tell, when she coyly confided, "Everybody does it, Custis. 'Fess up. Don't you ever close your eyes and pretend I'm somebody such as Sarah Bernhardt or Ellen Terry while you're having

19

your wicked way in my pedestrian pussy?"

He laughed and assured her, "Aw, your pussy ain't that bad, and I've already told you about the time I met Miss Sarah Bernhardt without screwing her."

It would have been unkind to let any woman know he'd have been willing to swap her and Sarah Bernhardt together for a crack at that lovely English actress Miss Ellen Terry. So he just kissed her some more and grabbed a fistful of Ellen Terry's tit. Only that didn't work because the real Ellen Terry was more willowy, with those fire-and-ice eyes staring honestly back at an admiring world in a way that made a man know she'd never talk this silly to any man lucky enough to get this close to her.

Meanwhile, there was nothing wrong with the bigger tits he had at his complete disposal. So he kissed the statuesque widow woman some more as he absently compared her anatomy with that of others he'd felt up in recent memory.

She was softer but actually thinner than that sassy Arapaho gal he'd been with the week before. She was bigger, in every way, than that poor harelip he'd wrestled with in that alley earlier that day. But Jesus H. Christ, why was he even thinking about a fully dressed woman that ugly when he actually had his old organ-grinder inside a gal who still turned heads along Sherman Street?

He kissed the widow woman again, as if to prove how pretty her upper lip still was. But after that he had to admit, with his eyes shut, old Splitlip Sally *had* felt mighty interesting from, say, the chin down. As he started moving in her again, the widow woman said that felt just right. He was glad she didn't say who it reminded her of. He decided he'd rather pretend she was Ellen Terry than a harelip married to a gargoyle. He doubted he'd ever see either of those gals again. That only proved, in the end, no man could know for certain what his future might have in store for him.

20

Chapter 3

By Monday morning Longarm wasn't the only one ready for some changes in his life. When he got to the federal building, a mite late and walking sort of stiff, Henry told him Marshal Vail was down the hall in Judge Dickerson's chambers with the prosecuting attorney's staff and a gone goose who wanted to talk turkey.

When Longarm joined them and took up a position against one oak-paneled wall, a mighty worried-looking humpback with an ashen ugly face was acting surprised the pickle-pussed Judge Dickerson wasn't anxious to cut cards with him.

It wasn't true Judge Dickerson of the Denver Federal District hung every defendant who appeared before him. He only hung 'em if the jury found 'em guilty. Longarm had often heard the firm but fair Judge Dickerson explain he didn't hang anyone for committing serious felonies. He hung 'em lest serious felonies be committed. So Longarm wasn't surprised to hear the crusty old judge tell Gargoyle Gibson, "You haven't anything to sell us, sir. I promise you a fair trial in any court I'll be presiding over. But everyone here knows you had a hand in stopping that Rowena stage, and it's a good thing for your wretched neck that nobody on either side died amid all that confusion!"

Marshal Vail just puffed on his evil-smelling stogie as one

of the prosecution staff opined, "It's a good thing for you we have no hard evidence on that wilder robbery down around Taos. For a witness was almost certain one of the raggedy bandits riding off after gunning the shotgun messenger was a humpbacked little son of a bitch!"

Gibson grinned sheepishly, a horrible sight, and replied, "I could give you the name of our leader who gunned that poor gent, if you gents were more willing to talk nice to a wayward youth who never meant serious harm."

Judge Dickerson exchanged looks with the three lawyers from the prosecuting attorney's office before he cautiously asked the prisoner, "Why would you want to be so good to us? I just told you there's no way in Heaven or Hell I can let you off with less than twenty at hard, no matter what you're willing to say or do."

Gibson nodded and replied, "I ain't asking for myself, Judge."

Dickerson was smart enough to follow the ugly outlaw's drift. He said, "It's for the jury to decide whether your wife just went along for the ride or helped you scout that feeder line for your gang, Gibson."

Gargoyle shook his ugly head and insisted, "No it ain't, Judge. None of us here are that green about the clockwork of the court. No jury has to decide nothing about my Sally if she don't get to be indicted, and you have my word I never told her all that much about my . . . horse-trading. That's the line I told her we was in whenever she asked where I was going, or where I'd just come from with another play-pretty for her."

Judge Dickerson glanced Longarm's way to quietly ask, "What do you think, Deputy Long?"

To which Longarm could only reply with a shrug, "They do say Jesse James has been seen at horse shows, claiming to be in that line under another name entirely. It's a good excuse for a strange face scouting the ways in or out of a county seat with a bank or more worth robbing. On the other hand, I'd be willing to bet my next pay envelope that Zerelda James née

Mimms has a pretty good idea what her husband really does for a living."

Gargoyle Gibson protested, "Well, of course *she* would. They say Zerelda James was Jesse's first cousin to start out with, and on top of that she's likely normal. You've seen poor Sally, Longarm. Did she look normal to you?"

Longarm repressed a shudder and replied, "Not hardly. But I can't say whether she was as *smart* as Zerelda James or not."

Judge Dickerson decided, "The unfortunate young woman's mental capacity is moot. The question is whether anyone can prove guilt or innocence in a court of law, gentlemen."

Even Longarm could see the boys on the prosecution team were a tad uncomfortable with that notion. So Judge Dickerson turned back to Gargoyle Gibson with a stern nod, saying, "Suppose we let your wife go for lack of evidence and still give you all the hard time we possibly can. Do we still have a deal?"

Gibson nodded soberly and replied, "It's a better deal than my so-called pards ever offered. I don't blame 'em for making tracks when Sally and me got picked up. I'd have done the same if Longarm there had spotted Shadowy Saunders in an out-of-the-way neighborhood during working hours, for Gawd's sake. But I'd have sure as shooting hired him a lawyer to bail him out, or at least got some tobacco in to him, before I lit out with all the damned money!"

He looked as if he was fixing to burst into tears, an awesome sight to contemplate, as he added with a sob, "The sons of bitches were holding most of the booty from that job up Rowena way while we waited for the serial numbers on them silver certificates to go stale. That's how come me and my poor Sally were living on bread and cold meat up above that stinky shop and all its glue pots."

Nobody else seemed to be picking up on what the humpback was leaving out, on purpose or not. So Longarm spoke up to demand in a firm flat tone, "Who's Shadowy Saunders, and why couldn't you and your woman have asked him not to boil

23

glue right under you if that cabinetmaking operation was just a cover?"

Gibson said, "They call James Hudson Shadowy Saunders because his mother's maiden name was Saunders and he don't come out much in broad daylight. You were right about me just scouting for the bunch. Shadowy Saunders or Jim Hudson was, or is, the mastermind. He's tall, dark, and skinny. Says his kin were Scotch-Irish, but a lot of folk take him for Spanish or Eye-talian."

Billy Vail told him to get to those mysterious Mexican woodworkers. So Gibson explained, "They was decoys. I told you Saunders was our mastermind. He bought a business that was up for sale with the profits of that Taos job. Hired real Mex woodworkers from a few counties south to look busy in case anyone like you gents came by. Had he bought a saddle shop he'd have had another crew cutting leather. The shop was just a place to store our guns and gear, along with me and poor Sally, partly to watch it and mostly because Saunders thought we looked too . . . distinguished to stay in the same rooming house with him and the others."

Vail asked Longarm how much of this he was taking down. Longarm had his notebook out by then but muttered, "Enough. It sounds like the usual self-serving bullshit to me. We don't have anybody called Shadowy Saunders or even Jim Hudson on our yellow sheets, and while I'm sure he's as fond of Splitlip Sally as he says, he hasn't really given us all that much."

Judge Dickerson agreed, saying, "A Sally in the hand is worth a gang in the bush, Mister Gibson."

The humpback whined, "What if I told you where Saunders and the others are likely headed, Judge?"

Judge Dickerson said that might be worth a Sally in the hand.

So Gibson said, "I can't say for certain where they'd be right now. But I know the next job Shadowy Saunders has in mind because I helped him plan it."

He saw Longarm had his stub pencil poised. So he licked

24

his thick lips and asked the judge, "I have your word she goes free, with no strings, Judge?"

Dickerson shook his head and replied, "Not unless you convince me you're telling us the truth. Deputy Long's not the only one in this room who's ever been sold a bottle of snake oil by a slicker about to go to trial."

Gargoyle Gibson shrugged and said, "Screw it. I'm ready to go back to my cell now if you gents don't want bigger fish to fry."

That sounded fair to Longarm. But Judge Dickerson said he was willing to listen to some evidence of integrity.

That was lawyer talk for dealing from the top, integrity.

Even Gargoyle Gibson knew how dumb that was. He said, "There's no way to prove my word before the boys stop another stage and likely get away again. Meanwhile, I got two cards faceup on the table, Judge. I want my wife off the hook, and you know nobody we know has lifted a damned finger to help either one of us. So what do you say?"

Dickerson said, "You haven't told us where your gang means to strike next yet."

Gibson nodded and flatly replied, "That's true, and I don't intend to till I have your own word she goes scot-free, Judge."

Dickerson swore under his breath, counted to perhaps ten, and snapped, "Done. I want you to take this all down, Deputy Long."

So Longarm did as Gargoyle Gibson said, "They're fixing to stop the Butterfield stage south of Shakespeare, in that Gadsden Panhandle of New Mexico Territory."

So Longarm said, "Bullshit. The Butterfield line runs way to the north of Shakespeare, if it still runs at all, and there ain't nothing south of Shakespeare, unless you want to count a stretch of Old Mexico that's too disgusting for most Mexicans."

Billy Vail paid attention to the wanted fliers that came in as well. So he was the one who volunteered, "We got a tip that fool Kid named after me was hiding out in Shakespeare with a gang of cow thieves. You remember that, don't you, Longarm?"

His senior deputy dryly remarked, "I do. Turned out to be some other saddle bum washing dishes for his keep in Shakespeare. Our Henry McCarty, Kid Antrim, or Billy the Kid is more likely closer to his old Lincoln County stamping grounds this spring. Meanwhile, like I just said, the Butterfield line don't get much closer to Shakespeare than the run over the divide betwixt Deming and Lordsburg, if the Southern Pacific ain't finished laying track in them parts yet."

Gargoyle Giboson protested, "You gents just ain't listening. We been stopping stages in the first place because all the stages left are packing payrolls and such through remoter parts, where a rider can be long gone before anybody ever hears about such a transaction. Butterfield still runs this spur line down through Shakespeare to a mining camp called Chrysolite, closer to the border. They haul the silver ore out across the desert by twenty-mule team as usual, but the mail and, more important, the miners' pay comes in by way of a twice-a-week stage, along a mighty lonesome desert road, if you follow my drift."

Longarm didn't follow it that far. He demanded, "Which way do they ride, once they stop that stage on the desert? You're right about how lonesome the country can get down yonder."

He explained to the Denver gents, "Mile and miles of dead flatland, spread like a dusty unwelcome mat on the border, between the Hatchet Range of the divide to the east and the even meaner Peloncillos to the west."

Billy Vail soberly added, "Apache Country, if you're lucky. The Yaqui don't range quite that far north *every* summer."

Longarm smiled thinly and said, "Hell, I never said this was *my* grand notion. I don't recall ever hearing about a mining camp called Chrysolite, south of Shakespeare."

Judge Dickerson, who heard a lot of mining cases, made a wry face and decided, "Chrysolite is a volcanic mineral and you find silver carbonate in the same sort of neighborhood. But the first thing I want to know is whether there's any such place mining any sort of rock where this defendant says there's

26

going to be a stage robbery. Then, if there is, I vote we drop the charges againt his wife and concentrate on preventing that robbery!"

Nobody else got to vote. So as soon as they found that damned mining camp in the damned gazetteer they sent Longarm to get that damned harelip out of the lockup across town.

Chapter 4

After three worried nights in a dreary cell, Splitlip Sally Gibson looked even less kissable than Longarm had recalled while kissing somebody more human-looking. It didn't help when she tried to grin at the good news he'd brought her. Then he got to lose an argument with the infernal property clerk while waiting for the pathetic sight to change from her prison smock to a now-somewhat-wilted summer outfit.

Unless Denver P.D. was lying, nobody had recovered the change purse she said she'd lost in that alley amid all the confusion, and the federal turnkeys said there was nothing on her release form to indicate they were supposed to turn over one dime from the wallet they were holding for her husband.

As he led her outside into the crisp morning sunshine, the veiled but disheveled-looking woman seemed more worried about her man than where her next meal and a place to lay her ugly head might be coming from.

Longarm explained, as he steered her toward the Union Depot for lack of a better place to aim, "Your Gaylord ain't likely to join you out here for quite some time, ma'am. If it's any comfort, he may have sacrificed a few more years of his life to free you. I don't want to hear how innocent you were to begin with. What's done is done, and the question before the house is where you better head from here. I got pals working for the railroad. So I could likely get you back to Utah Territory, if that's where you want to go."

She asked bitterly, "Why? The only folks in Utah who never treated me like a turd in their milk bucket are dead and buried. Lord only knows where my *real* folks went after they left me to die on a durned old salt flat."

Longarm said soothingly, "We ain't got no salt flat around here, Miss Sally. If you don't want me to bum you a train ride, we'd better see about finding you someplace to stay. I can't take you over to my rooming house across Cherry Creek because my landlady might not believe it's platonic. But I know this place just down the way, if you don't mind the sounds and smells of a Chinese laundry on the ground floor. We can get you a deal because some folks do."

He took her elbow to steer her the other way along Wynkoop as she asked him how he expected her to pay for room and board at any price. When he allowed he could let her have a half eagle to tide her over until she got some sort of job, she heaved a defeated little sigh and said, "Oh. Well, all right, if that's the way it has to be, and I reckon it does."

He hoped he wasn't following her drift as he led her to that place he knew where Wynkoop sort of ran on down into the sand flats along Cherry Creek. He bought her soda water to drink across the way while he dealt with a Chinaman who didn't cotton to white boarders as a rule. Longarm got along better with the Sons Of Han because he'd faced down a mob for them in this very part of town during those misnamed Chinese Riots of the '70s.

It hadn't been the Chinese who'd been rioting. A bully called Dennis Kearney had convinced a heap of other assholes that some Chinaman was sure to steal their jobs and run off with all their wives if they didn't get him first.

Old Chang Lai, who still hated most white folk, but had a fair mind as well as a long memory, agreed to put up with the ugly gal and feed her all the greens and rice she could eat for two bits a day or a buck and a half a week, which seemed fair enough. They shook on it. Then Longarm paid a month in advance and called the gal over. He admired Chang Lai's manners when the older man never let on she was so ugly.

Upstairs, above his laundry, Chang Lai left the two of them to settle up, or settle down, as they might see fit, in the one small but clean furnished room Longarm had hired. Longarm was reaching for his wallet once again when Splitlip Sally commenced to unbutton her bodice with a gallant sigh, asking him to at least be gentle with a woman who'd never been with such a big husky gent before.

Longarm said he hadn't either, and hauled out a ten-dollar silver certificate as he added, "You hadn't ought to flirt quite so convincingly, ma'am. There's some of us who just might believe you meant it."

By this time she had her bare shoulders and one tit uncovered as if to make up for her poor split-up face. Longarm told her to cut that out as he folded and tossed the bill on the bed, saying, "If you mean to linger here in Denver you're going to have to get a job pronto. A month's rent and that much spending money is all I can spare, and Lord only knows when if ever your incarcerated husband will be able to get at his own wallet."

Splitlip Sally let her bodice fall around her waist, displaying all her charms from there up as she fumbled at the drawstrings of her Dolly Varden, sobbing, "Nobody's ever offered me half that much before, but I'm still scared. You're so big and, well, I ain't sure my Gaylord would want me pleasuring the man who captured him. But it's a man's cruel world, so . . ."

"I sure wish you'd pay attention, ma'am," Longarm said as the damned fool married woman let her skirting fall around her ankles and stepped out of it in just her thigh-high black cotton stockings and high-button shoes to reach up and unpin her hair. Her raised elbows and warm cascade of soft wavy hair inspired him a heap more than her disfigured young face. He was commencing to see how even a man better looking than Gargoyle Gibson might just get it up for her after all. But as she sat down on the bed with her hair down and knees spread in resigned welcome, Longarm kept a firm grip on his own reins and remained standing. "It ain't high noon yet, and even if it was, my boss frowns on any of his deputies tampering with witnesses. That's what they call what you seem to be offering. Tampering. So no offense, I just can't tamper with you right now."

She looked sincerely confused as she demanded, "Then how *can* I pay you back for treating me so generously, Deputy Long?"

He said, "Most gals I've seen so much of call me Custis. But I did bring you here in my official capacity. I stood perfectly willing and able to put you aboard that train to Utah, as I said. But seeing you mean to loiter here in Denver for your man's trial and all, I figured I'd be a friend in need and see if we could sort of scratch one another's backs, see?"

She didn't. She turned over to climb atop the bed on hands and knees, thrusting her shapely derriere up at him, cheeks spread, as she demurely replied, "Go ahead and scratch all you like, as long as you don't draw blood."

He sighed and said sincerely, "Lord love you, that looks downright tempting, ma'am. But I thought I just explained I ain't allowed to tamper with you. What I mean was that your Gaylord tells us he's a little fish and I know Judge Dickerson can give more breaks than he let's on."

"What's the matter?" she demanded, wagging her shapely naked rump at him as she bitterly added, "You wouldn't have to kiss me, not screwing me in *this* position!"

He said, "I've noticed that, ma'am. So pay attention. Your man got you off by giving us the handle of his gang leader and where the gang means to strike next."

"Gaylord told me he deals in horseflesh when he has to go off on business for a day or so. He never said anything about a gang," she insisted, winking her rosebud rectum at him.

That looked tempting too. He'd long since figured one reason folks felt so deliciously dirty about each other's privates was the natural mix of delicious and disgusting smells and juices of the natural crotch. Even Ellen Terry pissed and

32

crapped just in front and a bare few inches behind what had to be the goal of many a man who'd be willing to marry her. A wicked damsel he'd met early on had confided she might not enjoy blowing the French horn half so much if her men friends didn't piss through the same swell instrument.

But hauling back on his reins by recalling how the other end of Sally drooled over exposed front teeth, Longarm insisted, "You'll be hurting your man more than covering for him if you insist on holding back, ma'am."

She sobbed, "Who's holding back! Go ahead and put it in, you big tease! I confess I'm starting to want some, now that I see you can be so nice. For I'm a naturally warm-hearted woman and they've had me sleeping alone three nights in a row!"

He sighed and said, "I ain't asking you to confess nothing the man you ought to be showing your bare ass to ain't already confessed to, ma'am. He admits that you were in his company scouting that Rowena stage just a few short weeks back. He said you didn't know Shadowy Saunders and the Scarecrow Gang were fixing to stop that stage a few days later near Trapper's Rock. But you surely must have met his so-called business associates, right?"

She shrugged her bare shoulders and shook both her ass and her head as she replied in an innocent tone, "I've met a few men Gaylord said he had business dealings with. One of them was mighty sneaky, as a matter of fact. His name was Jim, and I wouldn't put anything past *him* after the way he treated me that time my Gaylord had to leave Lyons for a few days."

Longarm asked if they might be talking about a tall dark skinny cuss called James Hudson when he wasn't being Shadowy Saunders.

She sort of sobbed, "That was him, Jim Hudson. He came over one night to talk sweet to me and even kiss me, on the mouth. Then all he wanted to do was screw me up my poor ass and then quit, just as I was starting to feel willing. I begged and pleaded with him to do it *right* to me before he went back to his own woman. But he said something mighty cruel about

33

my looks and just left me hanging there all a-throbbing!"

Longarm whistled softly and decided, "Everyone seems agreed a tall drink of water leading that raggedy gang is meaner than the rest of 'em. Do you reckon your husband could suspect his so-called business associate was given to corn-holing his wife while he was out of town?"

She explained in that maddeningly innocent voice, "Oh, Gaylord knows Jim screwed me up the ass that one time. Gaylord said he was sort of glad Jim left the rest of me so pure."

"Jesus H. Christ! You *told* your man?" Longarm marveled.

To which she calmly replied, "Gaylord and me have no secrets. A woman who screws behind her husband's back is committing adultery. I told Gaylord before we married up that I was warmer-natured than some gals he might have met, and he said he was glad."

Longarm smiled thinly and observed, "I can see why a man called Gargoyle might be. Getting back to his false friend, Jim. You say this born opportunist has a woman of his own?"

Splitlip Sally pouted. "Her name's Alice. Gaylord calls her Fat Alice, but I've never seen her. When Jim Hudson was abusing me he complained she was inclined to just lay there, like a side of beef. Maybe that's why Gaylord said to just forget it when I suggested he pay Jim back by abusing *her*."

So Longarm wasn't able to get much more than he'd already had for his time and money. He questioned her some more, and even got her to sit up straight as she retraced those travels she could remember with her man.

She confirmed some suspicions about another stage robbery up Wyoming way, sort of. What might or might not have happened on the trail as she ate chocolates in a Cheyenne hotel wouldn't have been enough to hang anyone even if a wife could be forced to testify against her husband. So he left within the hour, a few more not-too-interesting notes jotted down. Jesus H. Christ, the day was still young and here he strode with a raging hard-on he wouldn't be able to do anything decent about until after sundown!

Chapter 5

Longarm made it back to the Parthenon Saloon before the last of the boiled eggs and pickled pig's feet were gone. But none of the other regulars, a lot of them mining men, had ever heard tell of a mining camp near the border called Chrysolite, although a well-dressed lawyer down from Leadville to try a disputed claim at the nearby federal building did opine Chrysolite smelled like silver. He said the jadelike rock was better known as olivine when found in gemstone quality, or serpentine when weathered dull and softer.

Longarm didn't care, as long as it sounded as if they figured to have a serious hardrock payroll down that way. Gargoyle Gibson had said his gang planned on stealing cash, not silver ore. They had the infernal settlement listed in the gazetteer as being there. So the question on Longarm's mind was the percentage of high-paid hardrockers amid a three-figure population. No gang was likely to ride half that way through dry country with high summer coming on to steal the pay of common workmen, likely Mex, in that part of a recent real-estate transaction with Old Mexico. But a man blasting or even mucking in a hardrock mine rated two or three times what a cowhand made, or close to a thousand a year.

Washing down a dessert of white radish and red onion with the last of his needled beer, Longarm ambled back to the office, where Henry, playing teacher's pet as usual, was poring over a sheaf of railroad and stage coach timetables behind his big boxy typewriter. As Longarm came in Henry said, "I'm glad you're back. I can't figure out how to travel-order you from the D&RG to that Butterfield feeder line through Shakespeare and points south if I don't let you lay over, running up hotel bills the accounting office is likely to piss and moan about!"

Longarm smiled. "Just direct me to find the shortest route possible at six cents a mile and I'll be a sport about any detours or expenses, Henry. I wasn't planning on riding in by stage to begin with. I figured I'd bum a free ride down to Fort Bliss, requisition some riding and packing brutes, and sort of pussyfoot in from the east along the border."

Henry, who typed heaps of travel orders, said, "You're talking close to a hundred and fifty miles of mighty empty country, save for cactus and Apache, Longarm!"

The tall deputy nodded easily and replied, "I would have said something else if I'd meant something else, Henry. I ought to be able to find water in the Portrillo, Florida, and Hatchet Mountains this early in the year. Got to cross all three ranges in any case. Figuring thirty or forty miles a night, holing up by day in such uncertain surroundings . . ."

"Why?" Henry said. "That Butterfield mail stage makes it from Deming in one dawn-to-dusk run."

Longarm shrugged. "Lord willing and neither the creeks nor Apache rise. Meanwhile, we know Gargoyle Gibson scouted that other line up in the Front Range by riding it as a passenger a time or two, and I'll be switched if we ain't got old Gargoyle down at the house of detention right now. So how in thunder would you expect me to spot *another* scout for that damned gang before *he* spots *me*, even if we were rubbing knees face-to-face aboard the same infernal coach?"

Henry sheepishly allowed that he saw now why Longarm preferred to ease into Chrysolite more discreetly. But he still thought a cross-country pack trip from Fort Bliss was stretching discretion as far as discomfort, with time to dwell on how awful it felt.

Longarm said, "You just go ahead and type me down that old Gadsden Panhandle and I won't cuss you as I itch. Approaching the scene of the planned crime from an unusual angle ain't the least of the method in my madness. If and when they *do* stop that payroll a spit and a holler this side of the border, they're going to want to ride hard for somewhere safer, with a shit-house full of hot and bothered mining men chasing 'em!"

Henry nodded. "Sure they are. But don't it seem obvious a gang robbing a mail stage a short dash from the border would just dash across that border before anyone could posse up?"

Longarm shook his head and explained, "That might look smarter on your average map than across the real scenery involved. Shadowy Saunders doubtless hopes everyone will figure he and his raggedy bunch made a beeline for some hideout in the Sierra Madres, or even the Chihuahua desert down that way. But if you think we got rough and empty country on *our* side of that stretch of border, I got news for you about the desolation to the south."

"You mean there'd be no place to go?" asked Henry.

So Longarm explained. "Oh, there's water here and even a patch of grazing there, all of it occupied and hotly contested by the most ferocious Indians left on the North American continent, or by Mexicans desperate enough to dwell where our own Apache move with considerable caution. So unless Shadowy Saunders is a mighty mean Mex, and Gibson says he's Scotch-Irish, I'd expect a run east or west along the border to where an outlaw with a handy amount of cash might change into better duds and simply board a train for wherever he'd like to be next."

Henry said he could see that now, but asked why the Scarecrow Gang wouldn't just ride west toward, say, Tombstone.

Longarm nodded. "I'll figure they did unless I notice better reasons to beeline east toward El Paso, where I'd say most strangers could blend in easier waiting for a train out. If that less-settled ride from Chrysolite to El Paso strikes me as really tough, I'll naturally chase the sons of bitches toward Tombstone as soon as I hear they've stopped that stage."

Henry asked, "Might not it be better to arrest 'em *before* they grabbed that payroll?"

To which Longarm could only reply, "How? You just now mentioned a dawn-to-dusk run across unsettled hills and dales and none of us know what any of the raggedy rascals might look like!"

Marshal Vail had grumped in from his own lunch just in time to hear that last exchange. So as Longarm turned to greet him the old grump said, "You're wrong. Let's talk about it in the back and let Henry get some work done out here, dammit."

Longarm was willing. He followed his boss into Vail's darker paneled office and helped himself to a seat, uninvited, on his own side of the marshal's cluttered desk. For Billy Vail was not inclined to offer his deputies a seat, and Longarm wasn't about to stand like a kid in the principal's office or an army private in trouble. He'd tried being an army private one time and hadn't enjoyed it much.

Vail sat down on the far side, fuming cigar smoke as he rummaged through the papers on his desk, explaining, "We questioned Gibson some more after you'd left to get his woman out. He seemed mighty vague about names and numbers once he'd given us Shadowy Saunders. But I caught a slip about the two of 'em having met in prison, and the ugly little shit must have forgotten there was no great mystery about his own misspent youth!"

Vail found a mighty expensive-looking telegram, at day rates, and chortled, "Here it is. Came in from Leavenworth just before I went to lunch. Made my coffee and cake set sweeter than usual. Don't it feel grand to be told you're smarter than a damned lying crook?"

Longarm agreed it sure did, and asked what Leavenworth Prison had to say about Gargoyle Gibson and James Saunders Hudson.

Billy Vail pouted, "Aw, shit, you guessed. All right, they was in the same cell block back in '76. I'd already known

38

Gibson spent five years at hard in Leavenworth when I wired them. They confirmed he'd met Jim Hudson alias Shadowy Saunders there, like he'd told us. So get out your damn notebook and I'll describe the bastard some."

Longarm did as Billy Vail began. "Born in Nova Scotia back in '42, making him about your height and a little older. After that he resembles a Latin lover who's recently starved to death and ought to fall down anytime now. They let him out of prison early and deported him back to Canada because he's consumptive. The warden over to Leavenworth found it depressing to have a prisoner coughing blood all over everybody."

"He must have been faking it some." Longarm said. "A lunger that sick back when Custer still wore hair should have coughed his last by now, if he really *was* sick."

Vail sighed. "I wish you wouldn't try to teach us older dogs how to scratch an itch. If the son of a bitch had gone back to Canada and died like he was supposed to, he wouldn't be leading a gang of raggedy road agents down our way, would he?"

When Longarm didn't argue Vail went on. "His hair was black when they let him out. May be starting to streak by now, the way such hair can on a white man. His eyes are Apache brown and, oh, right, he's got a tattoo just above his left wrist that sometimes shows a tad when he's dealing cards. It's a coat of arms. An eagle bird in red with a single-masted galley boat in black superimposed on a gold shield."

Longarm nodded. "Sounds like a family coat of arms, and Gargoyle said he was Scotch-Irish. You said he hailed from Canada, where they take such notions more seriously, still having a queen and all."

Vail nodded. "Halifax, Nova Scotia. Only, they tell us him and his folks moved west to the prairie provinces while he was still little. He worked as a bronc-buster till he decided to steal for a living, and rode south into this land of more opportunity with the Mounties hot on his trail. He got his jolt in Leavenworth trying to steal stock from the U.S. Army Remount Service."

Longarm nodded and said, "He told Sally Gibson he was interested in horseflesh. I've heard how his condition can incline its victims to an unwholesome interest in flesh in general."

He brought Billy Vail up to date on his strange interlude with Gargoyle Gibson's harelipped wife.

When he finished Vail grimaced. "That explains why Gibson was willing to give us just that one name. No leader who'd mess with *my* old woman and leave me to rot in jail would be *this* child's leader very long! But you say Shadowy Saunders *has* a woman of his own?"

Longarm nodded soberly. "She's called Fat Alice. So who can say what a lunger with a raging hard-on might do with it to whom?"

Vail repressed a shudder and decided he'd as soon pass on either, adding, "I've seen the pathetic harelip. So Fat Alice must be a total balloon and ugly besides. But I'd rather kiss a fat gal with anything like a human face than that drooling Splitlip Sally!"

Longarm shrugged. "You ain't seen Miss Sally's bare ass. So don't write the other gal off as worse than, say, pleasingly obese. Horny men, just doing it for fun, are inclined to get horny over contrasts. So I can see how a horny lunger enjoying the charms of a pretty-faced fat gal might get to wondering what it felt like to brutalize an ugly-faced gal with a beautiful behind."

He lit a fresh cheroot. "He likely got some added pleasure out of doing a pal dirty behind his back. The harelip told me Saunders sent her man out of town on business for the gang before he calmly corn-holed her. She was pissed enough to tell Gargoyle when he got back. So, yep, I can see why Gargoyle might see fit to peach on such a two-faced pal."

Then he took a thoughtful drag on his cheroot and added, "That don't sell me the rest of his story, though. He said those Mexican cabinetmakers, or fake cabinetmakers, knew nothing about that payroll job down New Mexico way. You say you couldn't get him to describe any other gang member better?"

Vail nodded. "We know they could look like most any sort of cuss, once they've shed their masks and the loose raggedy duds they wear over their regular outfits. But what does it matter who Shadowy Saunders might be riding with, provided you spot him in time?"

Longarm said, "Might make a lot of difference, if Gargoyle was fibbing about those workmen nobody's seen since. The descriptions we got from Gargoyle, Leavenworth, and the folks who sold that property to a big fibber seem to match up. But I was just telling Henry I expected a beeline east or west along the border with an Anglo gang on my mind. All bets are off if even half the gang is Mex, or even worse, Yaqui!"

Billy Vail started to say something dumb. But since he already knew how many so-called Mexican border raiders were really Indians at heart, he could only suppress a shudder and say he hoped Gibson's story about those missing Mexicans had been true and that they weren't part of the gang. "I ain't about to let you invade Mexico again, Longarm. You know how upset our State Department gets every time you upset El Presidente Diaz with one of your declarations of war."

Longarm chuckled fondly at the memory of a fairly minor albeit full-scale battle with Los Federales down Baja way, but assured his boss, "Don't worry. Federales, rurales, and bandidos put together don't scare me half as much as riding into Yaqui country after a band of Yaqui!"

Vail frowned thoughtfully. "Why would they have to be Yaqui?"

Then, before Longarm could answer, the old ex-Ranger nodded. "Right. Neither Anglos nor Mexicans who didn't talk that Yaqui-Aztec dialect would have the chance of a snowball on a hot stove in Yaqui Country. If Saunders *should* be dumb enough to jump that stretch of border without Yaqui guides, just let him go and they'll take care of him for us. That's an order."

Longarm looked disgusted. "Why don't you order me not to stick my gun muzzle in my mouth and pull the trigger? You don't have to order a man not to commit suicide, do you?"

Vail shrugged. "Not as a rule. With a deputy like you, I can't afford to take nothing for granted."

Longarm snorted, "You're sure sending me one hell of a ways on the say-so of a self-confessed sneak. But I'll see if I can bum a ride aboard a southbound way freight come tomorrow morning."

"Don't want you bumming slow rides in the sweet by and by," his boss said. "Told Henry to ship you express this afternoon. I want you down yonder *before* they stop that stage, not *after,* you casual cuss!"

Longarm started to invent some excuse to leave town feeling a mite less frustrated. But old Billy Vail's wife was one of the very gossips that young widow woman up on the hill was so worried about. So it was likely safer to skin the cat another way.

He rose to his considerable height, saying he'd best see how Henry was coming with his travel orders, and when that didn't seem to draw any fire, he tossed in a casual remark about wiring his old Mountie pals up at Fort MacLeod for any additional shit they might have on consumptive Canadian crooks.

Billy Vail said that sounded like a good idea. So Longarm got out of there, trying not to grin like a shit-eating dog as Henry handed over his typed-up orders and travel vouchers.

Longarm had been raised to never lie flat out, if it could be avoided, so he really meant to send that wire to Crown Sergeant Foster up along the Oldman River, after he got his saddle and other possibles from his own quarters and checked them at the depot just in case anyone asked his landlady when he'd left. For it only stood to reason he'd have to wait until he got a reply from Fort MacLeod before he went tearing south. And as Billy Vail had often said himself, it was a scandal to spend five cents a word on day rates when Western Union was willing to give you a far better deal on night letters, sent after regular business hours when the telegraph lines might have otherwise hung idle.

Not wanting to pester his old pal Sergeant Foster earlier than he had to, Longarm ambled all the way to his hired digs, took his own sweet time before he strode back out with his heavy gear, and left it at Union Depot after betting the old-timer in charge of the baggage room it was impossible to check stuff in and out without leaving any record of the transaction.

After he'd lost a whole silver dollar and had more freedom of action, he ambled to the nearby Western Union and composed a night letter to his Mountie pals, asking for all they had on old Shadowy Saunders. The clerk behind the counter told him he'd be lucky if he got an answer before noon the next day. Longarm just nodded soberly and allowed a man just had to do what he had to do.

Now all he had to do was stay the hell off the streets until it was safe to spend at least one more night where he'd spent a swell weekend, one he looked back on with renewed inspiration.

He paid up, lit a fresh smoke, and strode back out into the afternoon sunlight feeling considerable anticipation for an after-sundown view of a shapely bare ass smiling up at him. That young widow woman was perhaps a bit broader across the hips as well as far prettier-faced than the naked lady he'd seen more recently down at Chang Lai's. But in a way, that only made the notion more interesting. He could see how a cuss enjoying the favors of a *really* broad-beamed pretty-face might find Splitlip Sally's swell little ass exciting, although a man would still have to be a total shit to corn-hole a pal's woman, even if she was pretty.

He warned himself not to dwell on female figures of any sort as a glance at the sky told him how many hours he had to kill before he dared go pussyfooting back up Capitol Hill. Killing time in downtown Denver was a lot easier when a man didn't have to consider bumping into folk who might bump into somebody from that damned federal building who might bump into Billy Vail later.

As if to prove his damned point, he spied one of the gals from the stenography office down the hall from Billy's office,

43

coming at him as he got to the corner of Nineteenth and Wazee. He could tell she'd spied him, and trying to duck someone you knew was as sure a way as there was to make them remember just when and where they'd seen you. So he pasted a pleased smile across his face and ticked his hat brim at her as they met up in front of a tea room near the corner.

Her name was Brenda Something, and he'd often admired the way her skirts swished as she passed by him in the marble halls. For she swished swell in her tailored skirts and form-fit bodice of summer-weight shantung. But a man was a fool to shit where he ate or act passionate where he picked up his pay. So Longarm tried to behave around such temptations and, so far, hadn't screwed more than a dozen-odd gals working anywhere near the federal building.

Brenda Something had on a bolero jacket that matched her coffee skirts, over her lighter ecru bodice. Her chestnut hair was pinned up under a perky hat of cream straw. So she'd have looked as if she might be going someplace even if she hadn't been toting a heavy-looking Gladstone bag.

Longarm found it was as heavy as it looked when he naturally took it from her to ask where they were headed with it. She protested as much as a lady was supposed to, and explained she had a train to catch. So Longarm confided he knew the way back to the depot, and as they retraced his steps together, Brenda Something told him she'd just been transferred to the Santa Fe District Court at a pay grade higher. But when he congratulated her, she said she had no pals in Santa Fe and wasn't sure she'd like it down yonder in New Mexico Territory.

Helping her across Wynkoop with his free hand, Longarm assured her, "Some parts of New Mexico might still be a mite wild, ma'am, but you'll like Santa Fe. It's a good old town, set pretty with the Sangre De Cristos smiling down from the east instead of the west, like here. I heard they were getting New Mexico more organized since General Lew Wallace got appointed governor and cleaned up that Santa Fe Ring. Which southbound do you have to catch, Miss Brenda?"

She said the three-fifteen and added, with a worried look, "I fear it may get me to Santa Fe after dark, and then what on earth will I ever do?"

He figured the time, nodded, and said, "You won't be halfway there by sundown, but we ought to have you in a nice hotel I know by midnight, Lord willing and we work that one transfer to the narrow-gauge side track right."

From her gasp of surprise he assumed she didn't read railroad timetables much. He explained, "We're talking better than three hundred miles with some of the mountain miles sort of twisty, Miss Brenda. But don't you worry, the D&RG has those new dining cars to serve us supper on the fly, and this hotel near the plaza stays open round the clock."

"Us? You mean the two of us, Deputy Long?" she asked.

To which he could only modestly reply, "My friends can call me Custis, Miss Brenda. I wasn't intimating anything forward about that hotel in Santa Fe. But I figured as long as we were both on our way south, and I know Santa Fe a mite better, I'd be less than a gent if I didn't escort you that far and see you safely bedded down for the night."

She dimpled up at him to confide, "I'm sure I'd feel far better arriving in a strange town with someone who knew his way around it. But where were you going just now if you were meaning to leave on the three-fifteen, ah, Custis?"

He smiled uncertainly and said, "Just walking around, I reckon. I'd lost track of the time. But now that I study on it, my office did tell me to get a move on. So ain't it lucky I ran into you?"

Chapter 6

Next to shooting fish in a barrel, nothing beat a long tedious train ride with a willing filly who soon had her fill of watching telegraph poles and mostly barren foothills whipping by outside. She found the scenery more interesting by moonlight after Longarm suggested a stroll back to the observation platform after sundown.

Longarm told himself Billy Vail would expect him to search for leads on the Scarecrow Gang in Santa Fe, seeing they'd stopped the Taos stage just a hard day's ride off. He didn't have to make any excuses to Brenda Something by that time. They'd come perilously close to doing it with their duds on, out on that platform, just before another couple, bless 'em, had come out to enjoy the receding moonlit tracks.

Longarm bet some Mex kids lounging around the Santa Fe depot they couldn't pack her big bag and his loaded-down McClellan to the Plaza Hotel for a nickel apiece. When he lost, Brenda asked how come he removed his Winchester to carry it personally. He said letting a total stranger stroll through the night with you could feel safer when you knew he didn't have sixteen rounds in the magazine to your five-in-the-wheel and a two-shot derringer. He was sorry he'd said that as soon as he saw the wide-eyed look she shot at the kids walking on ahead of them. But then he decided it might not have been so dumb when she commenced to cling so tight to his free arm he was glad that wasn't his gun hand comforting her.

She giggled and warned him to shift his hand a mite, lest she waste her passion, as she called it, out in public.

He'd stayed at the Plaza Hotel the last time he'd been in Santa Fe, although not with the same blushing bride. As he approached the clerk with a poker face, she admired a paper palm tree away from the lamplight near the front desk.

The elderly balding night clerk knew better than to comment as Longarm signed them in as a couple from Kansas called Jones. Longarm had explained the last time, flashing his badge, how a lawman had to be discreet when he was traveling about with a possible witness to a serious offense. So the older man simply assigned them a room and bath at the going rate for a double, dryly observing they got lots of couples named Jones, Smith, and such.

That reminded Longarm of his swell excuse for getting off a few miles short of El Paso. So without really hoping for much, he felt he ought to haul out his notebook, check for the date of that Taos stage robbery, and ask if they'd by any chance hired rooms to some mighty odd-looking Smiths and Joneses at around the same time. As he described a humpback traveling with a harelip and a tall thin drink of water with a taste for plump traveling companions, he was rewarded with an amused chuckle and, "Who could ever forget *that* bunch? There were eight couples in all. None of them named Smith or Jones, though. I'd have to look it up, but I believe that tall dark gent said he was a Captain Easton and that his bunch was a troupe of actors."

Longarm said they'd been acting indeed, and got out his pencil to take notes more sincerely as he asked for fuller descriptions for all but the gargoyle and the harelip, explaining he'd already had a good look at those two.

Brenda Something was commencing to pace back and forth near their piled baggage by the time Longarm had established Shadowy Saunders did seem to have some gray at his temples and that Fat Alice was a honey blonde as well as a right pretty gal with a right full figure. The night clerk figured she had to weigh two-fifty if she weighed an ounce.

Longarm guessed closer to an even two hundred pounds, hearing a six-foot man of two-fifty described as fairly fat, and seeing as how the skinny old night clerk recalled Fat Alice as average height for a woman.

Then he put his notes away and let a prissy bellboy tote their baggage up to the third floor for them. Not wanting to make a bad impression on the staff of such a fancy hotel, he tipped the kid a whole two bits.

Brenda Something was already clawing at her own duds as he got rid of the bellboy and trimmed the one lamp by the big brass bedstead. So Longarm leaned the Winchester against the bed table, made sure their door was bolted on the inside, and tried to beat such a fast undresser into bed.

He lost, of course. Brenda Something didn't have a gun rig to shuck and secure over a bedpost. So by the time he was out of his long underwear she was moaning and playing with her fool self atop the chenille bedspread. So to save her from going insane, as some said you surely would abusing your privates that way, he just got it in her deep enough, without bothering to shove a pillow under her sort of skinny hips. It worked all right after all, once she had her kneecaps firmly planted in his armpits, and they both came so fast he believed her when she sobbed she hadn't had any since she'd run off from a bad marriage back East almost two full years before.

She told him about the older gent she'd wed to get away from a strict home, but Longarm didn't ask what he'd done to displease her. He was sure he knew by the time she'd made him let her come on top, more than once, before confessing she just loved it dog-style on the rug.

Longarm said he could dog-style her faster, deeper if she let him do so his way, with her knees and elbows bouncing aboard those bedsprings. So that was the way they did it, and she sobbed aloud, while coming, that she really admired a masterful man who was polite enough to shove it all the way in and hold the pose for a lady as she throbbed her way back down from her fireworks display.

Then she made him sort of wonder who might be trying to master whom by demanding he leave it in there forever, or at least till they got hot enough to move some more.

He chuckled and told her to speak for herself as he let himself go in her at last with a dozen more serious thrusts. But once he'd let it rip he was considerate enough to remain standing, in the presence of a lady, and keep her spitted on his semi-erection by gripping a hipbone gently but firmly in each rough palm.

He could tell from her internal twitching that it felt comfortable to her as well. But by then they'd reached that less excited plane where a man who really liked women was just as glad he was with a real pal instead of a professional. For even when they were in the mood to talk in bed, whores never seemed to have anything as interesting to say as your average gal who didn't solve all life's little problems with her twat.

As if to prove his point, the warm-natured stenographer sort of nibbled his shaft with her warm wet innards, and casually asked him what all that stuff about strolling players had been about down at the desk. So Longarm told her, as he gently screwed her some more, about the case he was on.

Being a fellow employee of the Justice Department, she seemed sort of interested as, better yet, she screwed him back at that same easygoing pace. But Longarm had just been making small talk up behind her until she said she was Scotch, without any Irish, and that she thought it meant something that Shadowy Saunders liked to call himself Hudson, Easton, and such. She said her own clan was Munro and that, like lots of Scotch kids, she'd been brought up on tales of Highland feuding and fussing as much as she had King Arthur or the War Between the States.

When he said he'd met up with some feuding Scotch folks up on the North Range a spell back, and knew how serious they could be about somebody insulting their great-grandmother's cooking, Brenda said, "Saunders, Hudson, and Easton are all septs of Clan Donald."

So he turned her on her back to finish right, again, with both her knees hooked over his braced forearms, before he said he had to light the lamp and take some of this Scotch broth down.

She was a sport about it, and even shared a smoke with him, her thighs together, as she listed all the septs, or clan branches, of a clan too big for everyone in it to be called MacDonald. She told him they used names running the alphabet from Allan to Vurich, but that variations on Aosdan, a mighty important chief, were preferred by the ruling branch, the MacDonalds of the Islands.

Longarm allowed he could see how Aosdan could be twisted into Hudson, Hughston, Easton, Hutchinson, and such. When he asked how Saunders might fit in, she told him Saunders was how Scotch folk spelled Alexander, the handle of another famous MacDonald.

He wrote that down, commenting, "They do say he takes all that stuff serious enough to have a family coat of arms tattoed on his fool wrist."

When he described it she nodded soberly and said, "Oh, he must claim descent from the chiefs then. That red eagle and black galley on a gold shield are the arms of MacDonald of the Islands. You say he's a road agent, dear?"

Longarm nodded, taking his cheroot back from her as he told her, "Horse thief too. They say it happens in the best of families. So what sort of crimes do you folk from Clan Munro favor, kitten?"

She took the smoke back, snubbed it out, and trimmed the lamp again as she confided, "Crimes against nature. Now that we've sort of broken the ice with all this innocent screwing, what do you say we get really nice and dirty?"

Chapter 7

They might have managed as much as four hours' sleep before she figured another dirty way to wake a man up, and by the time they'd finished again, on the floor, it was broad-ass day outside.

Longarm had been wondering how he was going to phrase it. But he'd long since learned it was often best to let the pretty little things have the first say, and so she said, bless her, she had to report in early to her new job at the Santa Fe federal building.

He kissed her sincerely and faked some sweet sorrow when she confided she already had a boardinghouse in town lined up, and would move in that night after work. She didn't think they'd understand her bringing home gentleman callers.

When he offered to be a sport about her breakfast, she said she was afraid to inspire gossip that way, but assured him she would never forget how sweet he'd been to her.

So they parted friendly, by the back stairs, and Longarm saw he had plenty of time to catch that train from Denver he'd been fixing to before Dame Fortune and Brenda Munro had beckoned. The way freight had barely left the Denver yards, and wouldn't stop here in Santa Fe this side of lunchtime. So he went in to have a late breakfast in the hotel dining room.

He ordered two helpings of waffles and pork sausage in the hope of putting some spring back in his haunches. The waitress had some spring in her own, and wasn't bad if a man admired pouter pigeons or gals sort of built the same way. The chesty brunette said her name was Nancy and that she remembered that theatrical troupe well, because they'd been big tippers and the tall skinny gent in charge had said he'd sure like to put her on the stage, if only she'd let him see, upstairs, whether her figure was completely natural or not.

Longarm had been planning on catching that infernal train out in any case. But his thoughts must have shown, for she leaned way over and almost got maple syrup on her big tits as she confided, "It ain't that I'm stuck up, and I do get off at six. But he was sort of oily and had a wife besides."

Longarm asked, "Honey blonde with a pretty face and, ah, ample figure?"

Nancy nodded and said, "Her blond hair came out of a bottle if you ask me. She just laughed when he flirted with me right in front of them all!"

Longarm said, "Well, that's theater folk. Tell me more about the rest of the troupe. I ain't just nosey. I'm the law, and last night the room clerk out front only recalled the more freaky ones in any detail."

Nancy proved she paid attention to the table she waited on by describing all eight couples in better detail, although nothing she was able to tell him seemed unusual.

She recalled everyone but the somewhat older leader, and of course the poor Gibsons, as more natural-looking. Well dressed and soft-spoken for theater folk. She said two or three of the younger men could have been Spanish, meaning prosperous-looking Mexican in Santa Fe, but that she was only sure about a couple of their gals, who'd been dusky and dressed sort of flamenco.

As he had some mince pie with his breakfast coffee Longarm got a better handle on the way Shadowy Saunders and his Scarecrow Gang might operate.

First they'd established a respectable presence here in this respectable part of Santa Fe, not far from both the railroad and where you could watch that Taos stage coming in or going out.

Taos, a bit more than sixty miles up the same east bank of the Rio Grande, was either the oldest or newest settlement north of Old Mexico, depending on who you talked to.

The Taos Indians had built their pueblos there before other folks wearing war paint had started work on London Town. The Spanish had tacked on a mission and trading post much later, at the time some Pilgrim Fathers were trying to teach other Indians about a somewhat different Lord. But if there was one thing Anglo and Hispanic settlers agreed upon, it was uppity Indians. So when the Pueblos along the upper Rio Grande had risen against a Spanish governor in 1680, and killed the new gringo governor in 1847, they'd had some minié balls and manners pounded into 'em. So now a heap of white folks dwelt in and about the big Indian agency and the modest military outpost up Taos way.

That was why the Scarecrow Gang had stopped the north-bound to Taos with payroll money in its boot. Then they'd shot both lead mules before riding off so raggedy and rich. Longarm now figured the road agents had doubtless made it back to Santa Fe to change back to sissy theater-folk enjoying the evening promenade around the plaza by the time the crew and passengers of that stage had limped on in to Chimoyo and put out the word on the wire.

Leaving a dime by his plate for the helpful waitress, Longarm started over to the Western Union to put his more recent thoughts on the wire. But he never did. For on second thought he realized Billy Vail would only want to know what in thunder he was doing here in Santa Fe when he should be heading for Shakespeare and Chrysolite. And on third thought, wiring ahead to where they might turn up next would be as likely to tip Shadowy Saunders off as to trap him. For the skinny bastard didn't seem to scout ahead himself, and now that Gargoyle Gibson was locked up there was just no saying who or what they'd have scouting that Butterfield spur.

A half-dozen beers later Longarm was able to catch that southbound way freight, and it would have gotten him and his gear into El Paso that evening if he hadn't dropped off a few miles north, closer to Fort Bliss.

He toted his heavily laden army saddle through the south postern as the first stars were winking on up yonder in the cloudless West Texican sky. He knew it was a New Mexican sky just above the blood red horizon to his left. He was glad the spring rains from the far-off Gulf of Mexico had backed off for a spell, Lord willing and he didn't get gully-washed in the desert to the west by one of their rare but willing summer thunderstorms. The dry but not too dry time between late spring and high summer was the best time to beeline through some otherwise mighty desolate country along the border.

He found the remount officer he needed to talk to at the post officers' club, sipping suds after a hard day's work on his rump. Longarm had won arguments about government horseflesh with the fat-assed cavalry john before. But this time the remount officer wanted him to argue with his C.O.

The graying bird colonel was fortunately sipping his own suds at the far end of the cavernous 'dobe club, and better yet, they knew one another from the big Sioux Scare of '76. But when Longarm explained why he needed at least two well-shod and seasoned mounts to sneak him over to the Gadsden Panhandle, the bird colonel sighed and said, "It's your hair, to risk as you see fit. But I just hate to lose good cavalry brutes to the damned Apache, Deputy Long."

Longarm blinked and replied sincerely, "I'd heard the Nadéne, or so-called Apache, were behaving themselves this spring."

The old Indian fighter grimaced and declared, "A well-behaved Apache is a contradiction in terms. I know the B.I.A. says most of the Apache bands came in to be counted and pick

56

up their handouts this spring. But Victorio's sworn to 'make war forever' before he'll stand trial on those stock-raiding charges, and he's got at least two hundred surly Mescaleros and Chiricahuas backing him up between here and where you seem to think you're going!"

Longarm pursed his lips thoughtfully. "I'm headed due west, and old Victorio's Tularosa Valley range is off to the northeast of here, Colonel."

The army man snorted like a bull with a fly between its horns. "I just told you that baby-butchering Apache and his fiends incarnate were *off* the Tularosa Reservation, you fool! My men and I are on full alert to ride out after the sons of Satan the moment we get word where he might be. He was last heard from down in the Tres Castillos, south of the border but north of Chihuaha Town, butchering Mexican women and children for a change of pace. Lord knows he's butchered enough Anglo women and children, the heroic pissant. But he's been known to go after full-grown men he caught alone on the trail, backed by his two hundred braves, as such cowardly shits prefer to be called, so about those ponies . . ."

"I'd as soon borrow a brace of mules," Longarm decided. "We've likely seen the last of the spring rains and it does get dry betwixt the ranges to the west."

He produced some cheroots, saw nobody wanted any save for himself, and put all but one away again as he continued. "I reckon I can get through on horseback if you'd rather, though. I promised my boss, Marshal Vail, I'd stay north of the border down this way. Even if I did stray south of it on my way to the Butterfield spur, I'd be mighty unlikely to meet up with Victorio. You just said he was a mite timid, next to most of his nation, and I've no call to disagree, having met real Nadéne like Cochise in my misspent youth."

The bird colonel looked dubious. "What's to stop Victorio from ranging that far west? Neither we nor the Mexicans have any serious patrols out on the playas with the big dry due, and Victorio does have kissing kin around the San Carlos Agency a mite further west, remember?"

Longarm nodded and replied, "I suspicion Victorio remembers all the enemies he made over to San Carlos by busting his word to old John Clum, a hitherto mighty friendly Indian agent, and getting a heap of White Mountain boys thrown off the so-called Apache Police."

Then he lit his cheroot before adding, "I wouldn't be worried about Nadéne friends or enemies south of the border and west of, say, the Casas Grandes if I was Victorio. For Yaqui jump all outsiders, red or white, and we are talking Yaqui all along the Chihuahua-Sonora line."

The two cavalry officers exchanged thoughtful glances. Longarm just went on smiling with his cheroot gripped between his teeth at a jaunty angle as the bird colonel marveled, "You expect us to give your hair and two good mounts to the damn Yaqui as a gift on a silver platter?"

Longarm shook his head. "Not hardly. You just heard me tell you I have orders to stay *north* of the border, and the Yaqui hardly ever raid north of it. I suspect somebody must've told 'em the Mexicans get a boot out of that, and there's nothing Yaqui hate worse than Mexicans. This Yaqui gal I met one time assured me her folks were the last of those Aztec nations the old-time Spaniards thought they'd civilized with their crosses and cannon. But like I said, I wasn't planning on meeting up with any Yaqui this trip."

When neither officer answered, Longarm said more grimly, "I got to get over yonder, with or without your help. I reckon I'd manage some other way if I had to. Just like you boys ought to be able to manage explaining why you couldn't help a fellow federal employee, once my boss wires some old army buddies in Washington Town."

So the bird colonel told his remount officer to rustle up some riding stock for the blackmailing son of a bitch, and turned his back on them, as Longarm had suspected he might.

Over at the stables, the remount officer naturally tried to stick Longarm with a lame mare and a homicidal mule. But his heart wasn't really in it at that late hour. So by the time the remount officer was back with the boys at the officers' club,

58

Longarm was riding out the postern aboard one sturdy eight-year-old chestnut gelding and leading what seemed a twin.

He figured seasoned cavalry ponies could get him across desert range this early in the big dry. But first he needed far more grub and water, mostly water, for the three of them.

So he stayed east of the Rio Grande, or Rio Brazos if you were from Old Mexico, until he rode into Smelter Town between Fort Bliss and the outskirts of El Paso. The ore refineries that gave such a name to the town while painting the night skies above it a sullen shade of red were naturally kept going around the clock, and Spanish-speaking folk preferred to work by night and sleep by day to begin with. So there were plenty of stores open in Smelter Town, despite its otherwise modest size and grimy street lighting.

He reined in out front of the general store he'd dealt with the last time he'd been down that way, and tethered his army ponies to the iron-pipe hitch rail the Mex proprietors were so proud of. Then he drew his saddle gun from its boot lest it tempt passing sinners, and strode on in to see if they expected him to pay for fancy trimmings at retail prices.

The hefty old Mex behind the hardware counter recalled Longarm well enough to sob in mock sorrow, "Ay, mierda, there go all of my modest profits for the month. Pero for why that Winchester, Brazo Largo? Did not I tell you last time you could have anything but la ama de casa at cost, for to show respect to Tio Sam?"

Longarm, as Brazo Largo translated back from the Spanish, just chuckled fondly and replied, "Sin falta, and I still ain't paying a dime higher than the same shit sells for along Larimer in Denver, where storekeepers pay better than twice as much rent. I need me more gear than usual this time, Gordo. So, no me jodas and you'll sell me more shit than usual."

As the aptly nicknamed Gordo, or "Fats," begged him to point the Winchester some other way, Longarm noticed a sort of gray and shadowy Anglo drifting along the darker back wall like a wisp of cigar smoke. It wouldn't have been polite to ask right out who the hell he was and what he'd been up to

59

in a public facility. So Longarm just nodded his way, and the mysterious cuss didn't nod back as he simply floated on out into the darkness.

Longarm ran the stranger's face and dull gray riding duds through his mental files, thrice, before he shrugged and asked Gordo if he might have queered a sale. But the Mex replied, "Quien sabe? He had just stepped inside a few moments before yourself, Brazo Largo. Before I could ask him for why, you were looming in my doorway with that Winchester at port arms and he moved around to the other side of the stove, perhaps for to be courteous, or perhaps because of a certain shyness around a mariscal federale?"

Longarm said, "I'm only a deputy marshal, and if he's wanted he can't be all that famous yet. Be that as it may, I got to gear up for some rough and tedious riding, Gordo. So for openers, you'll be able to sell me a saddle pad and pack tree with some ten-gallon vulcanized water bags, if we're talking about fair profits and not opening the old umbrella once we get it up the gringo's culo."

Gordo held his fire till he'd heard how much cracked corn and canned grub Longarm wanted to pack along for himself and the two ponies. Then he named a price that inspired Longarm to suggest he elope to Infierno with the mother who'd raised him to be such a total pendejo raro.

Gordo naturally swore on the head of the same mother that he'd only quoted the prices they'd charged him for such luxuries, and so, in the end, they'd settled on far less and Longarm still said Gordo had no call to blame a West-By-God-Virginia boy for old Santa Anna losing so big to Sam Houston on the San Jacinto that time.

That many supplies and the gear to pack it added up to a fair-sized pile atop the counter. So Gordo said he'd fetch help from out back, and Longarm tagged along.

He wasn't lonesome. He'd just recalled old Gordo and his many kin dwelt across the backyard of this one story 'dobe business, and that a man could sidewind a few back doors down, unseen by anyone out front, if he had a mind to.

Longarm thought it was better to be safe than sorry, even when common sense said you were likely being silly as a schoolmarm peering under her bed for strange men.

That stranger in the dusty gray trail duds had been acting at least as strange as anyone your average schoolmarm noticed in or about her average schoolyard, and what the hell, if he wasn't up to anything he'd be long gone.

But he wasn't. Longarm had found it simple to excuse himself from old Gordo and circle through the darkness down past a few lampposts, across the street, and back up it in the inky shadows behind the stores until, sure enough, he spied that same mysterious rider covering the lamplit door of Gordo's vacated store from behind a big old cottonwood trunk on this side of the poorly lit thoroughfare.

His unknown enemy seemed intent on gunning him with that long-nosed Remington Dragoon Conversion he had cocked and trained on old Gordo's front door. So it would have been far safer to shoot first and ask questions later. But Longarm had noticed suspects answered a heap better when he questioned them alive and well. So he trained his Winchester's even longer barrel on the cuss from close behind and calmly told him, "Freeze in place and let that horse pistol fall wherever it has a mind to if you'd like to enjoy one more breath, you sneaky rascal."

The man behind the tree with a gun must have known who'd just addressed him in such a firm tone. He let go of the Remington and never moved a hair as, meanwhile, Longarm's tensed-up senses picked up the soft metallic snick of some other gun's safety catch.

So he wasn't there anymore as a shotgun blasted open a black slab of shadow behind him. For he'd spun out into the cinder-paved street to train his Winchester the other way, and fired an instant later as the sneak with the scattergun put a full double load of number-nine buck into his pal against the cottonwood.

Then he'd stepped out into better light to drop his smoking ten-gauge to the plank walk and belly flop down atop it, as anyone else might have with a round of .44-40 so close to his shock-frozen heart.

Longarm had reloaded and rolled both bodies faceup in the poor light by the time half the town, it seemed, had responded to those two fairly loud gunshots.

Longarm had cradled his Winchester over his left arm and pinned on his own badge with his free hand by the time he spied a cuss in the crowd packing a copper badge and a bull's-eye lantern. So he called out, "Over here, Constable. I'd be Deputy U.S. Marshal Custis Long, and I still have no idea who these sons of bitches I just shot it out with might have been!"

The local lawmen—there were three of them—had heard tell of Longarm, and didn't want to arrest him for defending his own life in Smelter Town as soon as they saw neither dead man was a resident.

Gazing down on their dead faces by lantern light didn't tell a lawman with a pretty good memory for faces a damned thing. Nobody but Gordo had even noticed the shabby strangers anywhere else in town before, and Gordo swore he'd only seen that one by the tree, just before Longarm had darkened his door.

But within minutes a town deputy had found a couple of dusty jaded cow ponies tethered closer to the next saloon up the way, and Longarm decided, "Let's try her this way, boys. Say these strange riders had just tore in from somewheres else, in a hurry to ride a mite farther. Like myself, they'd want lots of supplies if they'd been planning to ride west across all that nothing-much."

A town deputy who'd hunkered down on his spurs to go through the pockets of the dead man by the tree held up an open wallet as he opined, "They couldn't have been planning on paying for much, if this here Mister John Brown was the one sneaking around any store. He only had this eight whole dollars and fourteen cents in change on or about his whole person."

Another local had already identified the shotgun-toter as a Bob White who'd died less than ten dollars richer. So old

Gordo whistled softly and declared, "Esos cabrónes cagados were planning for to rob me! Madre de Dios, had not my salvador, El Brazo Largo, arrived just in time for to spoil their plans . . ."

Before the big fat Mex could hug him Longarm protested, "Let's not leap all over conclusions either! It works more than one way. This one I met across the way could have been shopping sincerely for no more than a buck's worth of whatever when I came in, and he recognized me as the law."

A local lawman pointed out, "You just said you never recognized him, Deputy Long."

To which Longarm could only modestly reply, "I might be just a tad more famous. This wouldn't be the first time I've had a wanted man throw down on me in the mistaken belief I wanted him."

The older and likely wiser of the three copper badges nudged the corpse by the tree with a thoughful toe and demanded, "So how come they didn't run for it?"

Longarm followed his drift. Then the old-timer went on to explain. "Say a pissant wanted by the law but not important enough to be recognized on sight bumps noses with a well-known lawman in a general store, shits his pants, and somehow gets outside again without getting arrested. Why in blue blazes would he and his lookout hang around another ten damned seconds? Wouldn't any outlaw with the brains of a gnat see it made more sense to run from someone like Longarm here than hang around and see what he might do next?"

A younger town deputy gasped, "Do Jesus, I surely admire what he did next to the sons of bitches, and you're right, Uncle Dan, they were fools not to ride like the wind the moment they larnt Longarm was within a day's ride of their pathetic asses!"

"Unless they were gunning for him to begin with," said a sardonic hatchet-faced cuss dressed like a cross between an undertaker and a prosperous rancher.

Longarm stared harder in the trick light as he soberly replied, "That's been known to happen too. I have been set up by hired gunslicks in my day, and it's a fact they hardly ever send a familiar face to gun a man unexpectedly."

Then he decided, "Well, like the old song goes, farther along we'll know more about it. Meanwhile, I got other fish to fry and I can't see frying 'em here in Smelter Town, no offense."

Nobody there had the rank on him to argue. So while the town law tidied up the mess across the street, Longarm and old Gordo's two oldest boys got the two army mounts loaded right to move on.

The willow-wood pack tree and trail supplies he'd just purchased added up to a slightly heavier load than Longarm and his own loaded McClellan as he started out. He knew the balance would tip the other way as they got ever closer to the Butterfield spur. But then and there he thought it only fair to load the supplies aboard the one gelding who hadn't carried much down from Fort Bliss, assuring the other, "I know you boys enjoy novelty as much as we do, and to tell the truth, I like to ride all my stock before I might be called on to ride serious. But we've wasted enough time here, and so we'd best get on across the damned old river and a few damned miles of what lies yonder before the sun comes up some more."

The ponies were in no position to argue. Gordo refused to take a nickel for the supplies, after all that arguing they'd enjoyed before the shootout. Old Gordo insisted, and Longarm had to agree, there was an outside chance he'd simply foiled a holdup. Some Mexicans could get mighty sentimental about such matters.

Chapter 8

Fording a river that late in the greenup didn't call for any
actual swimming. Longarm just removed his boots and rolled
his pants knee high before cussing himself and his brutes
across in the dark, through numbing snowmelt that swirled
halfway up a man's stirrup leathers and wet the bottoms of
his saddlebags.

After that the going got easy for a spell as they followed
the chalky wagon trace west by moonlight between wire- or
cactus-fenced produce fields to either side. It was too early
to tell just what might be sprouting in any particular field.
But it was safer to guess anyone fencing with wire had drilled
in a uniform planting of corn, beans, collards, or whatever.
The old-time local farmers of Mex or Mission-Breed descent
took the time to grow their self-repairing fences of prickly
pear, and spent a tad more time and thought on their planting. For they'd long since learned, in this harshly beautiful
valley, to work with an unforgiving sun rather than against
it.

Longarm was sure the smaller fields enclosed by cactus
windbreaks had been drilled so the stalks of red, white, and
blue corn would sprout first, providing shade for the squash
vines planted between corn rows and bean poles for the frijole
vines popping up between the stalks. They'd have marigolds,

peppers, or both growing every fifth or sixth row in place of the squash to discourage bugs, borers, and rabbits from working all that deep into a crop.

An Anglo nester could spend a small fortune out this way for Paris Green, Bordeaux Mixture, and such without getting any better results than the earlier farm folks got for free just by taking the time to study the country instead of challenging it to a duel.

Longarm studied the lay of the land around him as it gave way to overgrazed slopes and then chaparral a few short hours' ride to the west of the river's richer ribbon of bottomland. A greenhorn could get in more trouble traveling across such semi-desert than he could trying to homestead it. Grasshoppers eating you out or bankers coming to foreclose on a failed spread hardly ever killed you outright. But out in the unsettled parts of such uncertainly mapped country a careless traveler could get his fool self killed more ways than he could shake a stick at.

Next to dying of thirst, death by drowning was what you worried most about in these parts, followed by being struck by lightning or Indians, in that order.

Even greenhorns had heard about dying of thirst or being killed by Indians in what the War Department had down on its maps as the uncertainly outlined but certainly tense "Apacheria," where neither army personnel nor property was allowed out of sight of a military post without an armed escort.

But as Longarm had just told that bird colonel, with some conviction, he doubted anyone but Victorio was out in force so far this spring. So that left the mighty uncertain climate in these parts at this time of the year to really worry about.

In high summer there was no way to cross dry country but at night, with or without hostile human beings to avoid. For trying to cross a barren playa under a southwestern sun, which could really fry an egg on the sun-baked caliche within minutes, could kill you sooner and more certainly than any fellow sufferer of the Indian or bandido persuasion.

66

In the shorter, cooler, and far wetter winter, it was just the opposite. A traveler was far safer crossing such country in broad daylight, and to hell with any human enemies, so he could watch exactly where he was going. Those big flat open stretches were described as "playas," which meant beaches or tidal flats in Spanish, because that was what they could act like, given a sudden rain-soaking, and things could get worse in some places when a pilgrim busted through a thin sunbaked crust into a mixture of lye water and mighty deep gumbo.

Finding himself and his ponies atop a long mesquite-covered rise as the sky began to get rosy back to their east, Longarm turned off the trail, explaining to his mount, "Red sky in the morning, sailor take warning. You ain't exactly a sailboat, pard. But Lord knows where the next high ground may be ahead, and meanwhile we have met up with at least two mighty unfriendly strangers in these parts. So what say we make both the rainstorms and anyone else out to get us *work* at it."

Having neither the brains nor balls it took to really worry with, the two geldings seemed contented as cows in clover once Longarm had them unsaddled and tethered in a thick mesquite grove half a mile and a furlong north of the trail, atop that same high ground. The thorny twisted mesquites grew apple-tree tall along the ridge, telling tales of groundwater not too far down. They'd long since shed their sweet twisty pods of the previous fall. But stock savored the feathery green leaves and white flower spikes of late spring and early summer enough to risk the wicked thorns the ornery mesquite grew to guard them. So Longarm figured his ponies would have something to busy themselves with if he simply watered them and fed them light. He watered them heavier than he might have on the north range. This was no place to risk a bloated pony, and there was just no saying just how dry that parched cracked corn might be.

Having seen to the comfort of his stock, Longarm figured it was safe to build a small cookfire, with dry mesquite, in a cleared hollow just over the western crest of the ridge, in broad-ass day. For it was night fires a scouting enemy could make out for miles. Come daybreak, all you had to worry about was smoke, and just as he'd warned his pony earlier, that eastern sky was breaking as gray and ominous as it ever got in these parts.

Mesquite wood burned hot with little smoke. Such faint blue smoke as rose from his tiny fire in a fair-sized hollow drifted down-slope to the west, below the level of the shaggy treetops. So after he'd cursed the weather, unlike Mark Twain he did something about it.

Once he'd spread his bedding between two runtier mesquites and tented a tarp above them over the thorny branches, he filled a cookpot from one water bag and dropped a can of pork and beans in. He hung the pot over the fire on a dingle improvised from a couple of forked green branches, and moved back up to the ponies to explain, as he untethered them, "We're fixing to have us some desert lightning within the hour, pards. The trick is to move you down the lee slope just far enough. A drowned pony ain't anymore use to me than a sizzled one, see?"

They must not have, or perhaps it was the electricity in the air that made them hard to handle as he halfway led and halfway fought them down to another mesquite grove just to the southwest of his own shelter and simmering bedtime breakfast.

Once he had the stock browsing spring flowers some more, he was free to hunker and smoke between the fire and his bedding. Seeing the paper label on the bean can had floated loose by then, he was able to fish it out with a quick bare finger. But then he decided not to toss in any Arbuckle Brand coffee after all. He was already more awake than he wanted to be, facing a long rainy day huddled out of sight off the beaten path. Longarm was no slugabed when he had serious call to stay awake. When things tensed up he was able to stay awake and reasonably alert for seventy-two hours at a stretch. The trick when things were half tense, like just then, was to catch such sleep as you might have the chance to catch, and not just fret and fidget when common sense told you to just be still for a spell.

His empty gut rumbled, only to be answered, louder, by those big dark clouds looming ever higher in the morning sky toward the east. So there went any further thought about taking advantage of an unusually cool day. The land out ahead was desert, most of the time, because the prevailing west winds off the far Pacific were blocked by many a mountain range between there and here. But every now and again, such as now, the winds decided to blow the other way, up from the Gulf of Mexico, with the big tropical clouds dripping wet as warm bath sponges and no serious hills over that way to wipe their wet asses on until they got to the higher and usually drier basins and ranges of the southwest border lands.

The sudden storms inspired almost as much thunder and lightning as rain, Longarm knew. He'd heard that soggy south winds sweeping up the Atlantic coast to trip over the sudden ridges of New Jersey made that eastern state the champion place, in those parts, to get struck by summer lightning. As he fished out his warm can of pork and beans he decided he'd still rather be in New Jersey at that very moment. For dry lightning sizzled and banged not a furlong away along the ridge to lift all the hair on the nape of his neck and rattle the bones inside of him as it turned the mesquite it hit to a pile of smoldering kindling and a drifting cloud of toothpicks.

The unexpected lightning strike had almost made him drop the hot can. It had spooked someone else even more. Although the second time Longarm peered that way, from under the lowered brim of his hat, a greener hand to these parts might have assumed he'd just imagined that flash of white among the spinach-green chaparral while still dazzled by the blinding lightning.

On the other hand, heaps of folks down this way wore that same shade of creamy homespun cotton be they Mex, Pueblo, or wilder.

A sneak in the bushes going bare-legged in a loose cotton smock was inclined to talk Nadéne or one of the Pueblo dialects, while a cuss wearing cotton knee-length pants was more likely a Mex or a Yaqui. The infernal Yaqui dressed even more Mex than the Nadéne or so-called Apache, and got Mex bandidos blamed for all sorts of disgusting things no mere outlaw would be interested in wasting so much time on.

Something spit on Longarm's bare wrist. Then little wet tree frogs commenced a war dance around the brim of his Stetson. So he set the pork and beans to one side, busted open the Arbuckle, and tossed a fistful in the boiling pot as he called out in Spanish, "It's going to rain and I have pork and beans to share with you under my tent, unless you prefer to drown behind that yucca you think I can't see through."

He couldn't really see through the knee-high clump of what they called soap weed up Colorado way. But he could tell from the way the mesquite branches above it shifted that someone who savvied his Border Mex was crawfishing back with less skill than a serious Yaqui would have displayed gut-shot. So Longarm let his own six-gun be as he shouted, "You do as you like. I have to get out of this rain."

When he was under the canvas shelter he drew his double derringer and left it in his lap, to see what might happen next, as he sat cross-legged and opened the warm can of pork and beans with his pocket knife.

What happened next was an even closer lightning strike, followed by buckets of warm rain coming down fire and salt while, somewhere in the deluge, some woman was screaming fit to bust.

Longarm had to laugh as he made the poor thing out, crawling toward him on her hands and knees while the rain pounded her back, rinsed out her long black dangling hair, and spanked her cotton-skirted rump as it bounced along after the rest of her. Longarm called out, "Aqui!" to aim her better as she scrambled his way sobbing, "Ay, Dios mio . . . que pendejada! Nos vamos a morir todos! Is the end of the world, no?"

As he hauled her in beside him he said in Spanish, "I'd say it looked more like an all-day storm. My fire has been drowned, but maybe the water will stay hot long enough to brew that coffee out there."

She turned over to sit up beside him, sopping wet, and regard him with her big sloe eyes, as dark as sin in a pretty little moon face tanned to a slightly lighter shade than his old army saddle. Her silver concho belt and coyote-tooth necklace told him, better than her plain white pleated skirts and shin-high deer-hide footwear, she was what the B.I.A. and War Department defined as pure Apache.

Knowing such critters usually came in sets, Longarm nodded at her and, still speaking Spanish, commenced to tell her who he was and how he'd always got along so well with Cochise, Eskiminzin, and other swell Nadéne.

She switched the conversation to English, saying, "Neither of us is a fucking scalp-buying greaser, and I learned your tongue when Taglito started that school for us at San Carlos."

Longarm smiled uncertainly at her and allowed, "You sure must have studied hard. Ain't Taglito what your kith and kin decided to call Tom Jeffords of the Butterfield Line and later the B.I.A.?"

When she agreed and said he could call her Nozan, he cautiously asked, "Ain't we both a good ways from your reservation if you're a White Mountain Chiricahua, Miss Nozan?"

The sopping-wet young thing commenced to peel her wet cotton off as if it had been itchy sunburnt skin, saying, "My husband and some other Chiricahua decided a few summers ago to ride with Victorio. I don't know why. Every time I asked my husband he struck me. Husbands don't like to be asked questions they may be uncomfortable with."

Longarm whistled softly. "You deserted that big war party Victorio's leading somewhere distant, I hope?"

She tossed her wet blouse aside and began to unfasten her concho belt and tooth necklace, all that was covering her firm tawny breasts, as she answered simply, "They're raiding down along the eastern slopes of the Sierra Madre by now, I think. My husband was killed over a month ago in a brush with the Mexican cavalry near Guzman. I did not want to ride with another fool. So one night I slipped away on a horse my own man had stolen to begin with. It gave out under me two days ago. I have been walking ever since. San Carlos seems to be farther off than I remembered."

He said he'd see about that coffee now. She didn't ask why he pocketed that derringer and hauled his Winchester out into the rain after him. He didn't have to ask how she'd run her stolen pony to death. That was the way her kind rode. Despite the sentimental bull gents like Ned Buntline wrote about noble savages, some Indians had no more consideration for their mounts than some whites. The Cayuse were inclined to pet their ponies as much as Ned Buntline figured a noble savage ought to. Comanche and Shoshone treated their stock as decent as your average cowhand might. But Lakota, Cheyenne, and the other Horse Nations rode their mounts rougher and stole fresh ones as they wore them out. As for the Nadéne, a pony was as likely to get eaten as ridden. A Nadéne preferred to fight afoot and only thought of a horse as handy transportation, as long as he wasn't expected to waste much time on caring for the critter. Nadéne women could be expected to know even less about caring for horses their menfolk stole. The Nadéne wouldn't steal so many horses, Longarm was sure, if they knew shit about the caring for them.

By the time he'd dragged his Winchester and the pot of weak and tepid coffee back under the dripping canvas, Longarm was soaked to the skin and the pretty little savage was sitting there noble and naked as a jay, as if they were old friends indeed.

Longarm had spent enough friendly time among Indians of more than one nation to wonder some about which side might have the dumber notions about modesty.

Most every white adult from Queen Victoria down knew just what lay hidden under all those stuffy duds, and most of them enjoyed fooling with such private delights every damn chance they got. So it was sort of silly, when you studied on it, to worry about even a flash of bare flesh unless you were invited to go to bed with it and kiss it all over.

Few if any Quill Indians kissed, or even felt one another up, worth mention, as they lounged around almost bare-ass in public and naked at home, sharing a quick piece of ass as free and easy as a white couple might share popcorn. So maybe, when you got right down to why white gals wore so much and behaved so shy, it was because they enjoyed fucking more than noble savages did.

Not sure about present company yet, Longarm dipped a tin cup in the watery coffee and announced, "I don't reckon this is worth it save as a wash-down, Miss Nozan. I see you've already started on the pork and beans."

She had indeed and wanted more. So Longarm reached in a saddlebag to the rear of their shelter to bring out a fresh can, along with some tomato preserves, saying, "I was only killing time with that fire to begin with. The main reason cow outfits stock up on canned beans and tomato preserves is that a body can eat 'em out along the trail cold, without noticing all that much difference."

The Nadéne girl agreed canned goods tasted just as filling if one inhaled them direct from the can. From the way she inhaled he suspected she hadn't been eating anything for some time.

But he called a halt once she'd consumed a can and a half of pork and beans, washed down with half a can of tomato preserves and all the coffee-tainted water she wanted. The tomato juice and boiled water would likely keep her from suffering anything worse than some comical tunes from all those beans. He was too delicate to explain such chemistry to even an Indian lady, but had he felt the need to, he'd have told her you had to break your belly in to digesting beans.

Old service men who ate beans most every night seldom farted any more than average. Trail drivers only farted a lot the first week or so along the trail. But a gal consuming a can and a half in one sitting, after not having eaten beans or much of anything else for days, figured to match the thunder outside with some heroic noises of her own before this stormy day was done.

He lit a smoke. It wasn't easy. That damned rain had soaked on through most everything, and it was a good thing he carried

73

waterproof wax matches imported from Old Mexico. Nozan admired such a a delicate brand when he shared the three-for-a-nickel cheroot with her, but asked if he wasn't afraid of catching a chill in all those wet duds.

He started to say something mighty stupid about the broad if somewhat gray daylight all around. Then, since she was sitting there wearing nothing but coyote teeth and her fresh-bathed tawny hide, he allowed he had been planning to get undressed and under the covers they were sitting on before she'd come along to sit on them with him.

So she said, "Dika! Let us get under the covers and warm one another up. I am freezing and I was afraid you would never ask!"

So he slid his rump over and let her slide her little bare body in ahead of him so he could peel out of his own wet duds, facing the other way, as the rain came down, the wind howled through the swaying branches over them, and another bolt of lighting hit just as he was sliding his gooseflesh naked body in beside her warmer and drier brown flesh. So she grabbed him, whimpering something in her own lingo that didn't really matter as she pulled his naked chest down against her warm firm breasts, sobbing, "I am afraid of the sky spirits. My mother was struck by lightning, gathering piñon in the White Mountains when I was little. I saw her dead face when my uncles brought her down. She looked as if she had been cooked on a spit and, oh, White Eyes, put it in and make me not afraid!"

He said his friends called him Custis as he acceded to her request by simply letting the rest of his old organ-grinder follow its own fool head, once she'd guided it through the hairless gates of her happy humping ground.

She wrapped her muscular brown thighs around his naked waist and giggled when he was all the way in, saying his pubic hair tickled. So he didn't ask whether the gents of her nation plucked their hair or not. He knew it was a myth that Indians just couldn't grow beards or body hair. The simple facts of the matter were the average Indian had somewhat thicker hair all over, but spread a good deal farther apart than your average white. So, seeing a thin growth of black bristles could look less tidy than a well-trimmed beard or mustache, Indians tended to just pluck such hairs as soon as they sprouted. But those who cared to could grow hair on their faces, or at least between their legs, as ugly as any white folk. So he was glad little Nozan hadn't wanted to. He had hair enough for the two of them down yonder as he slid his naked shaft in and out of her childish-looking but mighty womanly twat. He could tell she was making it feel that tight on purpose, bless her, even before she moved her bare feet up to run her toes through his damp hair and beg him to shove it in to where she could taste it with the base of her tongue.

When that didn't work, and he couldn't keep it up anymore for her without a damned break, she decided to taste it with the base of her tongue the easy way. Her moist pursed lips felt swell on it as well as she proved they could get it up some more after all. So the rainy morning in a bedroll turned out mighty enjoyable after all.

Then, all of a sudden, with Longarm dreaming they'd been doing it dog-style out in the rain, he awoke with a start to realize that storm had blown over, an afternoon sun was blazing down around the edge of the tarp above from a clear cobalt sky, and Jesus H. Christ, he'd fallen asleep in the naked arms of a paid-up member in good standing of the Chiricahua Nation!

Worse yet, he'd woken up alone. So propping himself up on one bare elbow to take stock of the situation, Longarm told himself in no uncertain terms out loud, "If you ain't the asshole of this entire world I can't think of anyone a flea's lick dumber! You're supposed to *screw* strange women, even white ones, not fall *asleep* with 'em, you poor trusting shit!"

But on further reflection he realized his missing Nadéne bedmate had neither slit his throat nor stolen his guns and wallet, which she'd had every chance to do, Lord love her. So maybe she was only passing some of those beans off in the chaparral, and once she got back he'd be able to screw her some more.

He sat up, shoving down the now-somewhat-stuffy covers as he groped for another smoke, idly noting as he did so that she hadn't left her Indian duds in there with him. But that only stood to reason, it being mid-afternoon atop a ridge all bristled up with mesquite and other thorny chaparral. The sensitive little gal would hardly risk her bare ass, or feet, in sticker-brush, would she?

That reminded Longarm he could do with a leak himself. So he slid into the denim riding jeans he'd been meaning to change into on the trail in any case, hauled on fresh socks and the same old stovepipe boots, and rose bare-chested with his cheroot gripped in his grin to tote only his Winchester into the brush with him a decent ways.

After he'd watered some already rain-soaked rabbit bush, Longarm returned to the shelter, calling out for Nozan when he saw she hadn't come back yet.

When he got no answer he headed down-slope toward those ponies he'd tethered securely in that mesquite grove. He felt more sick than surprised when he saw, at a glance, she'd helped herself to one army mount and a heap of supplies, including every water bag.

He punched a tree trunk hard. When that didn't help he had to laugh and tell the pony she'd left him, "What the hell, she must have really loved me. She didn't kill either one of us, right?"

Chapter 9

First things coming first, the first thing Longarm did that afternoon was nothing much. It was already hot and getting ever hotter as the blazing white sun baked all that fresh moisture into the normally dry desert air. It felt bad enough lounging bare-ass in the shade. He knew Nozan would be feeling worse as she rode off to perdition with all his damned water. But she was used to such suffering and so there was an outside chance she'd make it on home.

It didn't matter to his mission whether she did or not. The only thing dumber than letting a Nadéne steal a horse from you would be to chase after them across Apacheria. For even if you had the time, and managed to cut the trail of an Indian who knew the range better, you stood a swell chance of catching up just as she'd met up with her own kith and kin. So, doubting many of her kind would treat him half so friendly, Longarm decided to chalk that pony and all those supplies up to experience.

Meanwhile he'd barely gotten started for the far-off Butterfield spur, and every time he thought about that he came up with an even meaner name for an otherwise great little lay. For like it or not, he was going to have to ride all the damned way back to the damned Rio Grande and start from scratch with fresh supplies and another damned pony!

It hurt like fire to even consider turning back. A real man was supposed to die before he'd turn back. But out this way a real man could wind up really dead instead of just talking about it.

Longarm had read somewhere about this famous explorer who'd done wonders and eaten cucumbers all over Africa or someplace without ever getting hurt or even having to eat a traveling companion because, he'd explained, he'd planned ahead and left more exciting adventures to the fools who hadn't.

Longarm figured he'd been sort of smug, since not *all* adventures happened to damned fools. But he'd just had one foolish adventure and didn't propose to have another, trying to prove he could punch on across Apacheria with one mount and a couple of small canteens.

"I swear I'll spit in old Gordo's eye if he dares to ask what might have happened to a whole damned gelding loaded with most of my damned trail supplies!" Longarm vowed, even as he knew he owed at least a few polite words of explanation.

The hell of it was, the closer to the truth he might get, the dumber he was going to look. An asshole who'd let a fully laden pack brute wander off in the dark looked bad enough. What excuse could any man give for falling asleep in bed with a Nadéne who'd admitted she'd been raiding for horses in Old Mexico with Victorio in the thieving flesh?

That afternoon he could only brew some really decent coffee and consume the next to last can of pork and beans after another stuffy nap under that sunbaked tarp. It hadn't really helped. He felt stiff and tired enough to sleep around the clock, alone, as he sipped black coffee in the sticky shade, shirtless, hating himself and the now-sullen red sun as he watched it slide down a cloudless sky bowl to the west.

He knew neither he nor his remaining pony would enjoy it if they turned back too soon. Aside from the heat sure to linger longer in such sticky air, the damned snakes would stay out later than usual after sundown. Just after sunrise or up to an hour after sundown were the usual times to get snake-bit in

78

this usually drier country. Snakes hunted, or struck at sudden surprises, when their cold blood coils were warm but not too warm. All that rain was likely to have flooded out the desert rodents snakes had an appetite for too. So his best bet would be to grin and bear it till, say, nine at least, and then ride back to take it all like a little man.

He tried to console himself by deciding it was just as well he had to retrace his dumb ride over range he already knew after all that rain. For late as it was getting, crossing wet desert was a lot safer winter-style by day.

"I should have let Henry send me the easy way," he'd just told himself when, somewhere in the distance, he heard a cavalry bugle.

He figured it had to be a cavalry bugle because who else would be signaling to spread enough riders to need a bugle out in line for a skirmish?

Longarm muttered, "What the hell . . ." as he hastily donned his shirt and put on his hat and gun rig, rising to such a mysterious occasion from his shelter and legging it up to the long crest of the ridge between him and all that tooting for a better look-see.

What he saw from the wooded crest, spread north and south on the greaswood flat to his east, was a full troop of cavalry coming at him at an ominous saber trot in a line of skirmish!

That only added up to a little over a hundred yellow-legs in army blue, fanned out in four platoons made up of three eight-man squads. But that skirmish line was dressed down neat and serious with sabers drawn. So Longarm broke cover, firing and twirling his Winchester clear of the mesquite on the eastern slope to let them see they weren't advancing on a possible Indian ambush after all.

The bugle froze everyone in place, swords glittering in the red evening sunlight. After a time two riders rode forward from the long blue line. One had a white kerchief fluttering from his sword blade over his head as they loped up to where Longarm waited bemused. As they got closer he saw the one waving the parley signal was a colored master sergeant. The other was a white kid wearing the gilt bars of a second john. Longarm wasn't at all surprised. He called out, "I don't know who you soldiers blue think I am. But I'd still be Deputy U.S. Marshal Custis Long and there ain't nobody up this way right now but me, Lieutenant."

The kid cavalry officer reined in to call back, "In that case you won't mind if I secure the area, sir. Carry on, Sergeant Clay."

The somewhat older and far burlier master sergeant nodded at Longarm as he lowered his sword blade and then, since each grown man knew exactly what the other was thinking, rode on past Longarm to vanish among the trees. Meanwhile, the baby-faced second john explained in a not unreasonable tone, "We'd be from the Fourth Cav, en route to Silver Creek in the Arizona Territory, and with all due respect, sir, we were told just this afternoon about Apache being spotted over this way!"

Longarm nodded and said, "I just talked to one this morning. If she was the same one you heard about she was headed home on her own. Said the main force of hostiles was still way off to the southeast, almost directly behind you all."

The burly master sergeant came back, reined in, and nodded at Longarm as he told his officer, "One pony and a one-man camp just over the ridge, sir. Horse and saddle both government issue."

Longarm said, "I'm government issue as well. Now I'm going to show you my badge and identification to prove I ain't no Apache."

As he got out his wallet with his free hand to flash it open at them he added, "Now I'm going back to where I just spent some mighty tedious hours waiting for it to get this cool. I have to break camp, load up the little I got, and head back the way you've all just come."

Then he turned on his heel and strode back up-slope into the trees, muttering to himself about the peacetime army. They were going to wear themselves to a frazzle long before they got to the Arizona Territory if they scouted every rise ahead of them as if the Army of Virginia might be trying to hold it. The sensible way to move in column through Indian country was to move your damned column around forty miles a day with outriders scouting at least a quarter mile ahead and out to either flank. But for some dumb reason the army either dismissed the danger of an ambush, the way Custer had, or worried about an Indian sniper armed with a scope-sighted .50-110 under every rabbit bush.

Neither extreme made sense, Longarm recalled, as he tossed the top tarp to one side and hunkered down to tidy up and tightly roll his bedding. For he'd learned the hard way, scouting everything in war paint from Arapaho to Zuni, that the American Indian was about as smart or dumb and as brave or cowardly as everyone else. It was true each nation had its own style of fighting, until the situation might call for some other way of fighting. The basic rules of the deadly game, as followed by both sides, called for watching out for your own ass while trying to shoot the other son of a bitch in the liver and lights. Experienced fighters of any nation would grab any edge a greenhorn gave them. But not even a contrary Comanche out for another coup feather was likely to attack a whole cavalry troop moving halfway professionally across country this open.

Longarm had finished packing and put on his gunbelt and denim jacket when that same young officer busted through the mesquite at him with a somewhat older white man mounted on a Morgan bay. The second john introduced him as Captain Sydney, which seemed fair enough. Then the captain told Longarm he had to ride with them as a civilian scout who knew the way west, which he didn't.

Longarm smiled up at the older man and explained, "You've caught me at a bad time, Captain. I was on my way to the Gadsden Panhandle, as a matter of fact, when I lost most of my trail supplies and . . . even worse, my water bags. So I'll be riding back to pick up some more this evening. You don't need no scout to tell you there's no water fit for man nor beast between here and the Portrillo Range, say, half a night's ride from here."

Captain Sydney said stiffly, "We don't advance after dark in Apache country. Once my junior officers report this entire rise has been secured we'll make camp for the night on this classic example of high ground. I'm taking every opportunity along the way to pound such rules into my recent graduates from the Point."

Longarm caught the second john almost grinning as he quietly observed, "I reckon nobody ever mentioned high ground while they spent four years at West Point, Captain. The Portillos are still around twenty miles off, day or night. Don't let anyone water his mount or top his canteen with such water as you're apt to find puddled out on the flats between hither and yon. I don't say *all* of it's poisoned with mineral salts from the rocky rises all around, but desert water is a lot like mushrooms. It's best not to sample either unless you know for certain what you're dealing with."

The squadron commander glanced down at the bedroll and saddlebags near Longarm's feet. "You may as well bed down in this place I see you've already chosen. We can talk about poisonous water and the weeds we've been warned about as well while you're riding with us after sunrise."

The younger officer had to look away as Longarm asked his C.O., "Have you been chewing loco weed already, Captain? I just told you I don't have a day's supply of grub and my one pony drinks five times as much water as the three of us."

"We have plenty of water," the captain said. "You'll naturally draw fodder and rations along with the rest of us, and you did say you'd already started for the Arizona Territory when you found you'd run out, right?"

Longarm started to argue, wondered why he'd want to do a dumb thing like that, and cautiously replied, "Well, they do say there can be safety in numbers, and I was aiming to get as far as the Butterfield spur alive as well as discreet."

The captain nodded curtly and said it was settled then.

Longarm said, "Hold on. I hope you understand I can't guide you and your command any farther than, say, Shakespeare, New Mexico."

Sydney shrugged and replied, "If we can pick up as good a guide in this Shakespeare, you'll be free to drop out of this column. If we can't, you won't. It's as simple as that."

Longarm took a deep breath, then decided to just swallow the mean words about a mother he'd never really met. For it was dumb to yell rape before you'd figured whether you were enjoying it or not, and the dumb prick had just now said he'd enjoy fodder, food, and water as far as he wanted to go along with this dumb joke.

92 4275

Chapter 10

Longarm felt better about falling in with the soldiers blue as soon as that bugle boy blew mess call, a tad later than usual that evening.

It had taken the mostly experienced colored troopers and their mostly spanking-new white officers the better part of an hour to set up their field bivouac amongst the mesquites. They had to cut a few down to line everything up the way Captain Sydney wanted it. He called it "roughing it in the field."

That was his name for not bothering with pitching tents under a desert sky so clear you felt tempted to reach up and catch stars like they were fireflies. But to give a fussy devil his due, the ponies were unsaddled, rubbed down, watered, and fed before even the officers got to spread their bedrolls in the cool shade of that evening.

Their late mess was served warm and well seasoned by a jolly old three-striper who allowed, when complimented, he'd cooked for some gentry of quality in his misspent youth as a house slave on a Tidewater plantation.

Longarm suspected that left to themselves most of the colored troopers might have preferred grits and gravy to bully beef and desecrated potatoes. He knew *he* would have. But the jolly old mess sergeant had let the dried spuds soak a spell and tossed in some canned cow before making his potato pancakes, and a few chunks of sowbelly tossed in with that bully beef did a lot to help such canned stringy shit imitate real meat of some kind.

Their coffee was downright good, brewed scientifically in a sort of potlike still so that it didn't matter if it was Arbuckle Brand or not. Coffee didn't need to be roasted and ground to exact trail-drive specifications when it wasn't apt to be boiled in a can on a cow-chip fire.

Longarm went easy on the army coffee, good as it was. For even though he was tired despite such a long lazy day in a bake oven, it was early and he just hated to wake up at four in the morning with nobody to play with.

He was naturally invited to mess, smoke, and jaw around the one officers' fire in the center of the camp. It sounded like more fun down the line where somebody was plunking a banjo and singing about his pretty quadroon. But since Longarm was not only white but a man who seemed to know the country ahead far better, they even served him some mighty fine bourbon with his after-supper smoke. Once he'd shown Longarm who was boss, it seemed Captain Syndey had calmed down to just holding court around the fire, looking smug, and not letting on whether he knew or not as his junior officers—there were five of them—pestered Longarm with questions about the great beyond beyond the greasewood flat to their west.

Longarm repeated what he'd said about water, and talked about the north-south ranges they'd be coming to no more than a hard day's ride apart all the way west.

He explained, "The Ho—you'd call 'em Digger Indians—say that in the beginning Real Bear, the grizzly spirit, clawed all of the dry lands out this way from north to south. A geologist gal I met up with one time had a more complicated story, but it's still a heap easier to find your way in Apacheria if you remember most any distant range you can spot ought to be running more or less north to south. They got mountains running east to west out California way, but you

86

boys are only headed far as the Arizona Territory, so what the hell."

He sipped some more bourbon from his tin cup. "I doubt you'll learn how hot and dry it can get out here before you and your men are settled in at Silver Creek. Save for crusted-over mud traps and more poison water holes than usual, this would be the best time to cross such country. You ought to see the crest of the late spring flowering by the time you reach Silver Creek. Desert flowers make up for all the dry times by sprouting, growing, flowering, and going to seed in the time it takes a few inches of rain to dry up and blow away."

The second john who'd ridden ahead to question him earlier was a Second Lieutenant Thornbury, and he seemed far more worried about the Apache he'd heard so much about than smelling flowers, judging by some of the questions he asked. Thornbury didn't seem to want to hear Victorio was off raiding Mexico to the southeast, or that most of the Nadéne off to the west seemed to be acting as well behaved as anyone could expect Nadéne to act.

Longarm explained, "They never called themselves Apache when they wandered down here out of Canada, about the time Columbus was getting as lost his ownself. Apache is a Pima word, meaning something between 'enemy' and that word you hadn't better call any gentleman of color unless you want him sore as hell at you."

Young Thornbury nodded. "The red devils certainly live up to that name, from all I've heard of their sheer delight in fiendish torture!"

Another young officer, in this case a first john called Warren, said flatly, "That's unfair, Thorny. George Armstrong Custer, in that field manuel he wrote on fighting Indians, warned against our judging them by our own standards."

The kid almost struck a pose as he droned on. "We may be called upon to subdue them, but it's only fair to remember that the Indian is only fighting for what he regards as his own land and his own way of life!"

Longarm might have stayed out of it had not Warren asked him if that wasn't the simple truth.

Longarm sighed and reached under his denim jacket for a fresh cheroot as he replied, "There ain't nothing simple about the Indian Problem, as Washington insists on calling such a sad situation."

He lit his smoke and shook out the match before he continued. "Folks who admire noble savages do 'em a smug disservice by lumping 'em all together and pontificating about The American Indian as if they were speaking, uninvited, for one family or even one entire nation. The first thing you notice, if you really study up on Indians, is that they come at you with different tongues, customs, notions, and intent. Even the Lakota and their Cheyenne allies are as different as we are from the Mexicans, while the farming Pueblo nations have about as much in common with Nadéne raiders as, say, an old-time German peasant and Attila's Huns."

He blew a thoughtful smoke ring toward the dying fire and went on. "As to the ways of life old boys like Victorio hold in such a high regard, I've heard Frank and Jesse James feel it's their own God-given right to stop a train or hold up a bank most any time the spirit moves 'em. Ask all the other nations who were in these parts first about their own ways of life, which included being raided or worse by wandering bands from the north who'd never learned to get by in dry country without robbing those who had."

Captain Sydney took the fat cigar out of his own mouth to ask, "Can I take it your thesis is that these Nadéne are no more than a criminal clan of Digger Indians, incapable of changing?"

Longarm shook his head. "Kit Carson already got a good three quarters of 'em to change by kicking the shit out of 'em back in '63, marching 'em to Fort Sumner and making 'em plant peach trees and hoe corn till they saw the light. We call the bands who signed up with the B.I.A. in '68 and got to go home the Navajo. They've changed a lot since the Pueblos first called 'em that. Navajo means 'them as

88

steal from the fields.' Nowadays Navajo grow their own corn and raise lots of sheep to pay for the silver they admire so much."

Lieutenant Warren objected. "Come now, everyone knows the Navajo and Apache are completely different tribes."

Longarm shrugged. "They are now. The ones we don't get to shoot on sight were capable of change, like Captain Sydney here suggested. The more stubborn ones we still call Apache seem partways there."

He took a drag on his cheroot and explained. "After the Nadéne under Mangas Colorado, Delshay, Eskiminzin, Cochise, and such said the Navajo bands were woman-hearted for signing that treaty of '68, a tough cuss called Tom Jeffords contracted to pack mail between Fort Bowie and Tucson. Jeffords and his riders shot it out so often with the Chiricahua Nadéne under Cochise that they somehow wound up on speaking terms. Old Cochise named Jeffords Taglito because of his red beard, and there's more than one version as to just how Taglito and Cochise worked out a deal. Some folks over in Tucson say Jeffords was brave enough to beard the wolf in his very den and convince Cochise he was getting too old for such kid stuff, while others hold Jeffords just paid tribute to a robber baron who was smart enough not to torture a golden goose to death. But either way, I should hardly have to tell you army men how your own General Howard parleyed Taglito's toehold into the famous Broken Arrow Treaty of '72."

Captain Sydney, busting a gut pretending he already knew, asked, "What difference did that leave between so-called Apache and the so-called Navajo once both had agreed to behave?"

Longarm said flatly, "Behavior. I just told you how the bulk of a sort of Gypsy nation switched to more peaceable ways as soon as they could see more profit in trading with others than raiding 'em. The dozen or so Nadéne clans we still call Apache have taken a sort of zigzag middle road, trying to make it as food-gatherers, hunters, and horse-breeders, with government handouts and some old bad habits taking up the slack. A fair but firmer Indian agent by the name of John Clum tamed Eskiminzin back in '75 by giving him the simple choice of behaving on an irrigated agency along the Gila or languishing indefinitely under army guard at Fort Grant. I hear both Jeffords and Clum have now quit in disgust with both sides. Ain't sure what become of Taglito. Hear John Clum has just started a newspaper over in Tombstone. Be that as it may, a good many Apache Nadéne have been trying to behave more sensibly, while some wilder ones called Victorio, Naiche, Nana, Loco, and such have been bitching about their B.I.A. handouts and avenging themselves on Washington by stealing nuns and raping horses in Old Mexico. I doubt you'll meet any of 'em doing anything the way we seem to be headed. The hunting will be better in the White Mountains this time of the year, and there's nothing much to steal this side of the Butterfield spur."

Captain Sydney cast a glance about, as if to make sure none of his colored enlisted men were pissing within earshot, before he said, "Let's hope you're right. I've just taken over this troop, and they do say Victorio alone rides at the head of two hundred seasoned desert warriors!"

Longarm laughed incredulously. "Suffering snakes, *Comanche* seldom attack army regulars they don't outnumber better than two to one, Captain, and Victorio's said to avoid any open contact with the Mex rurales or rangers. Like I said, he's out to steal nuns and rape horses, not to fight with armed and dangerous white eyes."

Young Thornbury laughed sort of wildly and declared, "By George, I suppose you *could* call a colored trooper a white eyes, from the perspective of a wild Apache. But just between us white men, how do you think our darkies will act under fire when the time comes?"

Longarm shrugged. "Like soldiers. Some of 'em as brave as the situation calls for, others acting like total cowards, most behaving halfways between. I reckon all you soldiers blue got to read that notorious ordnance report put out sort of secretly just after the Battle of Gettysburg?"

Captain Sydney must have. He looked away, muttering all that was ancient history, involving green troops. But young Thornbury asked what Gettysburg had to do with colored troops. So Longarm smiled thinly and replied, "I don't think there could have been all that many at Gettysburg. I was talking about the Union Iron Brigade that stood up to and stopped Pickett's charge in its tracks with what the newspapers described as a deadly hail of musket fire."

Young Warren said, "They described it correctly. I've seen the photographs Brady took right after the battle. The slopes in front of the Iron Brigade positions were littered with rebel dead."

Longarm nodded soberly. "General Meade noticed. So he ordered full reports on just how much ammunition every one of his men still had left, with a view to replacing it."

Captain Sydney muttered, "Now see here, even in a battle as serious as Gettysburg a good number of troops are held in reserve."

Longarm said, "I'm only speaking of the Iron Brigade. That thin blue line that held Cemetery Ridge against the best troops Lee had to throw at 'em. There's no argument those boys in blue stopped the boys in butternut cold. They say Lee bawled like a baby when he reviewed what was left of Pickett's division. But I was talking about how the average soldier behaves in battle. After that field inspection they held smack after Gettysburg, they found only half the soldiers who'd been in the thick of the action needed any new cartridges or caps because only half of 'em had ever fired a single shot."

The junior officers looked more surprised than Captain Sydney. So Longarm went on. "The more cheerful part is that nobody broke and ran from his assigned position and those who actually aimed at anybody aimed good enough. I see your troopers are packing Spencer carbines instead of them old single-shot rifled muskets the Iron Brigade did well enough with on Cemetery Ridge. So, hell, if even a third of 'em stand their ground with seven-shot repeaters and hit no more than half their targets, we're still talking about way more

91

than you have to drop to stop Indians as serious as Comanche or Cheyenne Crooked Lancers."

Thornbury seemed a worrisome cuss, even for a second john. For he objected, "I add your grim figures up to mayhaps a hundred and five crack shots before anyone has to reload, and they tell us that Victorio is leading more like two hundred mighty serious Indians."

Longarm shook his head. "I doubt two hundred raiders and all their dependents could live off the country well enough to stick together all that close. But even if they manage, Nadéne just don't fight that way. They don't give a warrior a coup feather for carrying on courageously in battle. They call any Nadéne who takes a chance or offers the other side any sort of break a total fool. Leaders like Victorio wouldn't stay leaders long if they took to ordering frontal assaults even on women and children. So if they do send you and your troopers after any Nadéne, you'll be lucky to get anywhere near 'em, and should you be so lucky, you'll likely find a hundred or so average fighters armed with seven-shot Spencers a fair match for any you corner. They ain't about to fight you unless you do corner 'em."

Captain Sydney stared thoughtfully at Longarm. "You talk a good campaign for a civilian, Deputy Long. You seem a a little young, but might you have been in the war by any chance?"

Longarm looked uncomfortable and replied, "I was a little young, and like you just implied, old war stories have a way of turning into old bore stories. So I reckon I'd best turn in now, before I get all wound up telling lies about some damned fool kids I used to know."

He was on his feet and bound for his bedroll before anyone there by the fire could even ask which side he'd ridden for. It wasn't as if he was ashamed of anything in particular he'd done as a fool kid who'd thought war might be fun. It was more the bittersweet memories of good friends lost suddenly and close calls that sounded a lot funnier later, which the smells and sounds of any army post or encampment always evoked in any man who'd ever been there.

As he got half undressed and slid into his own roll, glad he was this tired, a mellow tenor voice was crooning off a ways:

> Oh, my pretty quadroon,
> My flower who faded too soon,
> My heart's like the strings of my banjo,
> All broke for my pretty quadroon.

Longarm didn't know why he felt so sad about the poor colored gal. But he did. Or maybe it just didn't seem fair that any old boy who sang so pretty was liable to wind up dead, Nadéne-style.

Chapter 11

That bugle boy blew "Boots and Saddles" at sunrise, just after a hearty breakfast of flapjacks slathered with sorghum syrup and extra-strong reheated coffee. So Longarm volunteered to ride out on point a quarter mile ahead. The colored lance corporal out on point with him was a regular who naturally knew more about Indians than your average officer. He said he'd campaigned against Comanche and Kiowa in the Buffalo War of '70 or so. When he said he'd never yet killed anyone personally, Longarm figured he'd really been in action. You seemed to get the most exciting war stories from old-timers who'd actually been assigned to garrison duty.

They didn't cut sign of anything worth inflating into even half-assed war stories as they loped along in the crisp morning air with the outfit tagging along behind in a column of fours. The two-rutted trace wasn't dried out enough yet to send dust more than stirrup high, and given the safety in numbers, Longarm had to admit they'd make better time and not suffer too much crossing such country by daylight with the weather holding.

It warmed considerably as the morning wore on, of course, but a rider who'd passed this way in August would laugh at the puny heat the New Mexico sun could manage this early in the big dry.

The broad flats out to either side were as pretty right now as they ever got. Most of the chaparral to either side of the trace was really hediondilia, or greasewood. The Mex folk called all such brush chaparral whether it was really scrub oak or not. Thanks to all the spring rains, the greasewood was giving off creosote fumes in full yellow flower. The bunchier, shorter, yellow-flowered shit that smelled more like turpentine, closer to the wagon trace where it got harder to grow, was naturally called turpentine weed. Here and there you'd spot the tall pink flower spikes of canaigre or pretty clusters of desert bluebonnets. But the really spectacular show was put on by the dozen or more varieties of tunas or prickly pear they grew down this way.

Longarm had read somewhere they suspected all American cactus was descended from some relation of the wild rose that got lost in the desert and pulled that stunt Professor Darwin came up with back in '59. Be that as it may, the cactus flowers surely looked like roses and came in all the rose colors, from white through yellow to deep crimson, all at once around Longarm that morning.

The lily family had invented heaps of ways to grow in lands of mighty uncertain rains as well. Aside from the soap weed or yucca you found all over the West where it didn't rain more than, say, twenty inches a year, the dry range down this way sprouted more impressive sotol, lechuguilla, and that hero of the lily clan, the agave or century plant. But only a few yucca of any sort were in bloom any given spring. So the few they passed had to make up for it by real fireworks displays of creamy white to sundown orange, shooting way up high on big bean poles that were mostly pith and wouldn't last much longer than their seed pods took to dry up and blow away.

By noon they'd made it up into the Portrillos, where far taller mesquite and even real oak called for a slower pace and more serious scouting. But as Longarm had hoped, they found no sign to indicate anyone had passed through in serious numbers since the last rains, and better yet, there were limpid pools of clear rainwater amid the weathered rocks all around. A colored sergeant warned everyone to filter their fresher water through their yellow kerchiefs lest they wind up breeding fairy shrimp in their canteens. So Longarm didn't have to say anything.

Captain Sydney ordered his mess sergeant to issue cold rations for the troops while their mounts enjoyed some oats, needle grass, and a little rest in such noonday shade as there was atop the wind-swept ridge. Then it was boots and saddles some more with old Sydney bound and determined to reach the Floridas by nightfall.

So they did. That afternoon spent forging across flatter desert got less comfortable but never really dangerous, and the early Mex explorers had named the Sierra Florida with their handsome greenery and gardenlike running springs in mind. When Longarm pointed out how this natural campsite might appeal to most any big bunch on the move, the captain agreed a secure perimeter made sense. Better yet, nobody expected Longarm, as a civilian, to pull picket duty after dark. So that night he really got more sleep than a man in any shape really needed.

The next day on the trail went even better, although the trail began to peter out, with cheat, needle, and other dry country grass sprouting sassy from the wheel ruts where the spring rains soaked in deepest. But the Butterfield trail to the north was better traveled this far from any settlement, even when the papers weren't whipping up another Apache scare.

The fresh growth served to keep the dust down, and even better, the sky got overcast some more, cutting the heat out of the afternoon sky. So Captain Sydney set a pace they'd have never sustained had it been even High Plains hot, and Longarm got to worrying more about the U.S. Cav than Indians as the purple peaks of the Sierra Hacita, or Hatchet Mountains, loomed ever closer above the western horizon.

Left to his druthers, he'd have been aiming a tad south by this time to begin with. For no matter what a puffed-up officer felt the whole world owed him, Longarm just wasn't headed the same way once they were over the Hatchets. But each and

97

every time he mentioned this to the stuffy cuss—during, say, a trail break—Sydney made ominous remarks about desertion in time of war.

Longarm knew even serious Indian raids hardly qualified as a formal state of war, and nobody could accuse a civilian of deserting an army column in the field in any case. So he failed to see how they could court-martial him drumhead-style if he did just tell them to go to hell.

But on the other lonesome hand, Cockeyed Jack McCall had openly boasted of gunning old James Butler Hickok after a Deadwood judge and jury had declared him not guilty. So a Colorado judge and jury had tried him some more, found him guilty after all, and swung the back-shooting son of a bitch.

Every lawyer Longarm had ever asked agreed the hanging of Jack McCall had been unconstitutional as hell. But nobody had figured a way to bring the unconstitutionally hung braggart back to life. So a man had to study some before he told a troop commander to just go screw himself out in the middle of what that commander persisted in regarding as a battle area.

The Hatchets were a somewhat lower but aptly named extension of the Continental Divide. They turned into the Rocky Mountains to the north or the Sierra Madre Occidental down Mexico way. Right ahead they were trying to live up to their local name by imitating a jumble of monstrous stone axes driven into the spine of North America. The maze of canyons and draws between the confusion of bare stone crags was well watered this time of the year, with plenty of grass for their mounts and cool shade, cast by ever taller and greener sorts of trees, from desert willow to piñon and juniper, as the trail hairpinned ever higher for some pass over the main divide. Or so Longarm hoped.

They made camp in an easily defended high hollow, surrounded by rimrock, with a handy mountain tarn in the center for watering the stock once the mess sergeant had all he needed for their supper and breakfast beyond.

After dark, before moonrise, Longarm was sorely tempted to make the move he was afraid he was going to have to make sooner or later, unless he wanted to explain how in thunder he'd wound up in the Arizona Territory to a boss who was at least as mean as Captain Sydney. For he knew they'd be crossing that Butterfield spur, in the flat desert ahead, by broad-ass day, where a man would still be in sight from the column a good four or five miles out, not counting dust a determined pursuer could make out twice that far.

But he didn't do it. He told himself he'd never have a better chance to slip away. Then he told himself he'd never forgive his fool self if he found out later someone had put an arrow through some banjo just as it was busting for that pretty quadroon.

He decided to see if he could slip away once he saw this bunch as far as, say, the Peloncillos, on the far side of the Butterfield spur. That would take him a tad out of his way as the crows flew, but the soldiers would be able to follow the greener slopes of the Peloncillos north to the more traveled Lordsburg to Fort Bowie Trail, while he would be in better shape following the foothills south, with only his one pony and meagre food and water.

He was glad he'd decided that way the next afternoon, when they proved what that poetical Scotsman Bobby Burns had said about the best-laid plans of mice and men.

After riding down the western slopes of the Hatchets, they had to swing around the north end of a monstrous seasonal lake that thought it was a big old alkali flat most of the time. So knowing that was the way they'd be coming, a couple of army dispatch riders were camped along the playa in a pear flat waiting for the troops.

When Sydney's squadron came through their natural bottle-neck, they handed him a message from the Fourth Cav. His colonel wanted him to swing down the Butterfield spur and wait up in Shakespeare for some major out for Apache with the First Squadron of the three a peacetime cavalry regiment rated. They'd just heard, over at Silver Creek, how the Mex and U.S. Cavs had agreed to fight on the same side just this once, against the mutual menace of Victorio and his border jumpings.

Longarm figured it was about time such rascals lost the privilege of fighting for their own sacred homeland all over a Southwest other folks were already living more peaceably in now. The sudden change in Indian Policy saw him all the way south to Shakespeare, where he was able to part friendly with the soldiers blue and, better yet, get to a telegraph office.

While waiting for answers to the wires he sent to both Denver and Smelter Town, Longarm was able to buy more trail supplies and argue about hiring an extra pony from the one livery in the little desert town. The crusty old Anglo lady who bossed the livery, and a couple of Mex kids who laughed at her behind her back, said she'd never let him take one of her ponies as far south as Chrysolite without a ten-dollar deposit.

Longarm said, "I don't want to *buy* the critter, ma'am. I only need it to pack me and my trail supplies each way. We both know I can't ride any further south than a mining camp smack on the border, and I doubt I'll be doing all that much riding around once I get there."

He started to go on about his intentions regarding the Butterfield agents and town law in Chrysolite. But she stopped him with a sardonic cackle and announced, "Now I know you're loco en la cabeza and I'd better ask a twenty-dollar deposit. For Chrysolite is a company town that doesn't have much in the way of local law, and the Butterfield stages don't run that far south."

When he blinked and asked if she was sure about that, the old crone pointed out her open livery door and snapped, "Go ask 'em at the Butterfield corral if you think I'm lying. Shakespeare is the end of the line, such as it is. Anyone down Chrysolite way who needs to send or pick up any mail has to use the Shakespeare post office, same as anyone else dwelling outside our durned township."

Longarm took her up on it. When they told him the same tale at the nearby Butterfield layout he started for the sheriff's office down the other way. But then he thought twice, and retraced his steps to the Western Union to see if he might have something a mite more sensible to say.

He didn't. Smelter Town had wired back that the Texas Rangers were still working on the true names of those old boys he'd had such a mysterious time with across from Gordo's. His home office simply told him to keep up the good work. Billy Vail still thought they were talking about a stage robbery where no stage seemed to be running.

He wired his boss what he'd just been told, suggesting someone have a serious talk with Gargoyle Gibson. Then he did trudge down to the sheriff's office, letting his jaded pony rest some more in the shady livery up the other way.

Rank having its privileges, and the day commencing to heat up, the county sheriff wasn't there in the elected flesh. A wiry old cuss seated at a desk under a straw sombrero said he was a deputy. He got up to open a file drawer and pour drinks for them both as Longarm explained what he was doing there.

Handing the younger lawman a healthy tumbler of tequila, the old-timer flatly said, "You've been sent on a wild-goose chase, old son. Miz Weidmann, over to the livery, told you true about this being the end of the Butterfield spur, and that ain't saying much. It's only running thrice a week, and when we do ship serious dinero in their boot we have a dozen or so riders tag along as far as the railroad. This is the first we've heard of any Anglo road agents, but between all the damned greasers and Indians in these parts it pays to be a mite cautious."

Longarm asked about shipments from the company town of Chrysolite, a day's ride catty-corner across the flats. The local lawman poured himself a second shot as he explained, "Some mail comes through here. They move their crushed and washed but still raw ore to the west, over the Chiricahua to the smelters closer to Tucson."

He swallowed his tequila, regarded his empty glass thoughtfully, and decided, "Better not this early in the day. I ain't certain they've been shipping *any* ore in bulk from Chrysolite this spring. I do know they've been laying off help. Silver prices are down and one of their Cousin Jacks I was drinking with last month said he'd been mucking nothing but low grade for some time. Silver mines are like that, you know."

Longarm nodded, more puzzled by Gargoyle Gibson's tip than the infernal mining industry. Everyone knew a silver mine could be a marginal operation even closer to market in wetter country. Silver was far more common than gold, but unlike the more precious metal, it lurked in rich lodes close to the surface, or petered out suddenly to rock that was hardly worth bringing out of the shaft.

He didn't care. Gargoyle hadn't said shit about Shadowy Saunders stopping any ore wagons bound for the Arizona Territory. He'd bought his ugly wife's freedom with a pretty tale about a stage robbery in a mighty inconvenient part of the country!

When Longarm said as much, the old deputy in Shakespeare asked if he meant to go on back to Denver and pistol-whip the lying cuss. Longarm declared, "It's tempting. But seeing you and the Butterfield line's been warned, I'd best traipse down to Chrysolite and see if I can find out what in thunder the ugly little shit might have had in mind!"

Chapter 12

It would have felt tedious on a cooler day, but running circles in a tiny town sounded smarter than riding circles across a big old desert. So Longarm checked out the few leads he had in Shakespeare while the sun stood high that afternoon.

There was no point in pestering his army pals, camped north of town with their tents pitched for a serious stay, so he didn't. They told him back at the Western Union that the mining company had strung a single line from Shakespeare to Chrysolite at their own expense. When they told him they relayed messages in or out of the company town when and if there was someone at the other end, Longarm asked them to try. But the Shakespeare telegrapher said nobody seemed to care down yonder. He explained the mining company had a railroad desk key with a battery of wet cells they were inclined to forget to refill when the acid got low in such a high and dry climate. He recalled Western Union had relayed something to Chrysolite less than a week or so back and, when pressed, allowed it might have been a telegram from Denver. But he didn't have a written record and just couldn't remember what the message had been, or who might have sent it to whom. He explained, "I wasn't on the key my ownself. I only heard about it from our night man. He'll be coming on a little after suppertime, if you'd like to come back then."

Longarm said he wasn't sure he'd still be in town. Then he went back over to the Butterfield layout. Their Shakespeare agent was a bright-looking young Anglo-Mex who looked a lawman in the eye when he talked to him. But he still insisted his outfit hadn't run their coaches farther south for some time. When Longarm asked why anyone might call the spidery ruts down towards Chrysolite the Butterfield spur, the Shakespeare agent explained, "It was for a time, when the mines down that way first opened. Cousin Jacks and all their kith and kin needed rides for themselves and all their baggage, till they got settled in and, worse yet, dug closer to the bottom. Chrysolite was a flash in the pan, even for a silver camp. They ain't had half enough folks down yonder to justify a coach a month. That's why we ain't been sending none."

Longarm nodded soberly and said, "They told me much the same at Western Union and the sheriff's office. So how do you figure a gang of road agents ever got the notion they might want to stop a stage on its way to or from a dying town with no stage service?"

The Butterfield agent shrugged and replied, "I only schedule 'em. I don't rob 'em. What if they scouted that section of our line when business was brisker, just a little over a year ago?"

Longarm thought. "Possible. Things do change out our way, fast enough for some to lose track, as old George Armstrong Custer surely remarked the day he met way more than the thirty-odd Lakota he thought he was trailing."

He broke out a brace of cheroots, handed one to the agreeable Anglo-Mex, and got them both lit before he asked if there'd been any other riders through these parts ahead of him, asking so many dumb questions about stage lines to dying silver camps.

The Butterfield agent started to shake his head. Then he proved himself bright as Longarm had hoped by saying, "Hold on. There was this high-toned lady and her servants, both Mestizos, an hombre y mujer of the peon class. She was looking for coach passage down to Chrysolite for the three of them. I don't know how they finally managed to get there, if they ever did. I wasn't able to help them."

Longarm said, "You might have helped *me*. Some of the gang I was just talking about are said to be Mex, or even Indio, and they all seem to have regular gals, if not wives, riding with 'em."

The Butterfield agent said, "Makes more sense than fooling around with trail-town doxies who might turn a road agent in for the reward. But I just told you this particular lady was high-toned. Might have been Spanish. Surely what my sainted mother used to call sangre azul de linaje aristocracia. I would find it hard to picture her riding with an outlaw gang. After a *fox* perhaps, sidesaddle, but sticking up a stage-coach . . . ?"

Longarm smiled at the picture but pointed out, "They'd hardly be holding a grand ball in that dying border town. What if she was aiming more for somewhere on the far side of the border?"

The Butterfield agent, who looked Mex enough to know, shook his head and flatly stated, "I just told you she was a high-toned white lady of pure Spanish or mayhaps French persuasion. An Apache squaw would have to be out of her mind to ride south of Chrysolite into pure Yaqui country. I don't know what makes Yaqui so mean. My own kin on both sides have never managed to have a serious conversation with the murderous sons of bitches."

Longarm agreed the mysterious high-toned lady worked as well as maybe some mine supervisor's lady. Then, since he wasn't about to find out there in Shakespeare, he went back to argue with Miz Weidmann at the livery some more.

The ornery old bat finally agreed to sell him a damned old Spanish riding or packing mule for fifteen dollars. Better yet, as they settled up and she supervised her help while they helped Longarm load up the stock, *she* recalled that same high-toned white gal with the two Mestizo servants. She said the lady had bought three riding mules off her a few days back, paying handsomely, cash on the barrel head with no infernal bickering, and yep, they had said they were headed for Chrysolite.

After that she didn't know why, or what anyone's name might've been. She said she only worried about such trifles when they wanted to hire a mount for the day and she had to consider them coming back.

So Longarm settled for riding out of Shakespeare a bit after three in the afternoon, with the shadows longer and cooling the desert pavement enough for the lizards to skitter to either side of the wagon trace south.

He'd put his McClellan aboard that Spanish mule, partly because mules could tote better in dry heat and partly to give his old army pal from Fort Bliss a break after all they'd been through together the last few days.

He swapped mounts halfway there, so he rode in toward the winking lights of Chrysolite about an hour after sundown, if that was the company town of Chrysolite ahead.

He failed to see how it could be anything else. For as his map and the wagon ruts he was following agreed, the dinky settlement was nestled against the western flanks of the Hatchet range, as if to prove that whatever had formed the Continental Divide had wrung a long dotted line of silver ore, mostly a silver-lead-carbonite a greenhorn could mistake for black dirt, from somewhere deep in the guts of Old Mother Earth. Longarm tried to remember why so much pale green porphyry and jade green chrysolite lay over virgin silver lodes, like foam formed over beer in the vats. But he was paid to look for outlaws, not paydirt, and since everyone agreed they were only moving low grade in bulk out of the company town ahead, he'd no doubt do better asking questions about payrolls, company safes, and such.

As he rode in along the one main street of an even smaller town than he'd expected, Longarm decided a payroll robbery made more sense than stopping a stage that no longer ran or robbing a bank that they didn't seem to have along their two-block business district. He made out a livery, one hotel, and two saloons catty-corner across the dusty north-south street.

Light spilled out from both of them, but they only had a piano going, listlessly, in the one to his right.

He didn't care. He stopped out front of the livery, bet a full-blood four bits they couldn't water and fodder his two brutes, and after he'd lost, asked directions to such town law as they had. The Indian pointed to a light over a sort of barn down by an ore crusher's tipple, and explained the Chrysolite Mining & Land Company had its own hired police to deal with such trouble as they ever had in such a tedious little town.

Longarm thanked him and legged it on over to see how the company police felt about a rundown on everyone in town not directly on the company payroll, and should that lead nowhere, some kind of surveillance, which Longarm didn't think a lot of either.

That sort of barn turned out on closer inspection to serve as a company office building, dispensary, warehouse, and such. He found a ground-floor door marked "Security," and went in to find a pallid young squirt with buck teeth and red eyes reading at a desk. The magazine he put down with a toothy grin was printed in French. Longarm suspected the grinning cuss had been more interested in the pictures. It was a scandal what they let them print in France these days.

Longarm introduced himself, and started to explain what he was doing at this end of the Butterfield spur. The red-eyed squirt cut him off with, "We've been expecting you. Got the message just a day before the line went dead. Why don't you grab a seat while I go up the slope and fetch Pink Atwell. That's who's in charge of company security here, Pink Atwell."

He tore out past Longarm like a willing worker who kissed ass every chance he got. Longarm wondered if he was going to get as good a job once this town died.

The only seat worth grabbing in such a dinky office was that swivel chair behind the desk. Longarm had been raised to be too polite to do that. So he hooked a denim-clad rump over a corner of the desk and picked up the French magazine to see if it was one he'd already read. It wasn't. But the pictures at the front of the dozen-odd stories hinted at more than they let you see all the way. Maybe the French words were dirtier, if a body could read them.

He knew what a derriere was, and didn't "langue tremblant" mean something like a "quivering tongue"?

He was still working on whose quivering tongue was up which ass when that squirt barged back in with two older gents, a bright-eyed Mex, dressed Anglo and packing a Schofield .45, and an older cherry-beaked individual who dressed more like an undertaker and walked in that dignified way of the habitual drinker.

The older man introduced himself as the one and original Pink Atwell, as if he thought Longarm should have heard of him. The Mex was called Concho, but talked as normally as the rest of them as he held out a hand to shake.

When Longarm took it, rising from the corner of the desk as he did so, Concho got a two-fisted grip on his gun hand while old Pink whipped out a double-action Remington and the buck-toothed kid made as sudden a grab for Longarm's .44-40. So Longarm naturally yelled, "What's going on here? Didn't this red-eyed asshole pointing my own gun at me tell you I was federal law?"

Pink Atwell smiled smugly and replied, "Bunny told us who you *said* you were, Shadowy Saunders. I reckon you didn't know, when you cut our line somewheres between here and Shakespeare, that Marshal William Vail of the Denver District had already warned us you might be head our way, pretending to be one of his senior deputies!"

Longarm laughed incredulously as Bunny, damn his red eyes, took away his wallet, watch, and worse yet, pocket derringer. Knowing it was not the time for sudden moves or even hasty words, Longarm said, in a desperately reasonable tone, "I'm not pretending shit. If you gents would be good enough to read my identification carefully, you'll see it describes me to a T, while as for Shadowy Saunders, he's said to be way skinnier and consumptive besides!"

Pink Atwell nodded to Concho, who proceeded to handcuff Longarm as Atwell pontificated. "I reckon Marshal Vail would know what one of his own deputies would look like. He wired us to look out for a tall rangy cuss with dark hair, a heavy mustache, and gun-barrel-gray eyes. Said you might try to pass yourself off for a Deputy Long you bore a faint resemblance to while you set us up for a robbery."

"Robbery of what?" Longarm demanded. "I just got it from the Butterfield agent in Shakespeare that no coaches run down this way no more!"

Atwell smiled more broadly as he nodded and replied, "A lot *he* he knows, and you really must be slick as they say."

Concho volunteered, "I reckon you and your gang had no way in the world of hearing this silver camp's being shut down permanent, with everyone here due their last month's wages and a bonus for them the company just can't use at any of their other mines?"

"In paper money, by mail coach." Atwell sort of chortled. "That big a payroll would weigh too much for one trip in real specie."

Then he frowned and, changing moods in that sudden way of the habitual drinker, snapped, "I don't see why in the hell I'm wasting time and breath explaining a robbery to a robber! Concho, you and Bunny better lock this slippery son of a bitch in the explosives bunker for now. It should only take eight or twelve hours to get a rider to the Western Union in Shakespeare. So lock him up with a canteen, but don't fret yourselves about feeding the sneaky devil."

Concho nudged Longarm's floating rib with the muzzle of that .45 and said, "Let's go, sneaky devil. I'm pretty sure a concrete bunker made to hold in dynamite explosions ought to keep you safe for just a day or so."

Longarm sighed and said, "You boys are sure going to feel silly about this. Can't you see what they've done to us? My boss may be peculiar now and again, but he'd never in this world send a wire such as you just described. So try her this way. Say the real crooks in Denver, knowing I was on my way, wired a confederate down around Shakespeare, likely in code, and then he—"

"Move out, Saunders," said Atwell, turning his back on them to head back to wherever he'd left that bottle.

Concho said, not unkindly, "He means it. The bounty they have out on you reads dead or alive. So let's quit screwing around, hear?"

Chapter 13

With the possible exception of an ice age, there was no way to pass time slower than in solitary confinement in the dark. Longarm figured he'd been pacing eleven feet, each way, for several hours when the boiler-plate door of the dank concrete bunker swung open to dazzle him with the brilliant glare of a miner's safety lamp.

The security man called Concho had the lamp on a tray that was piled sort of neighborly, despite that Schofield .45 in a free fist. Longarm made plenty of room as the young Mex stepped in, kicked the door shut, and told Longarm to grab the damned tray.

As Longarm did so, Concho locked the door after him and set the lamp on a stack of stout boxes in the corner. Longarm hoped they were empty. The lettering on 'em read "Hercules 60% Nitro."

He saw there was a pot of coffee, a bowl of chili con carne, and a plate of tortillas, with the tin cup and horn spoon it took to consume it all with no danger to oneself or others. As he moved with the tray to a seat on another dynamite box, he told Concho this would doubtless be recorded by the angels if he ever had anything to say about it.

Concho put his .45 back in its low-slung waxed holster and lit a smoke, oblivious to the faint headachy odor of nitro in the bunker, as he modestly replied, "Don't hurt to offer a man a last smoke before you blindfold him. Either way, I've been thinking, and I'd like to think I'm at least as smart as an old fart who got fired from the Pinkertons for drinking on the job. The wanted fliers on you, or at least on Shadowy Saunders alias Hudson, give Canada as your place of birth."

Longarm poured a cup of coffee, not minding the chickory smell of the shit at all, as he replied, "Leave us not forget I'd look a mite less lively if I'd been let out of prison as a consumptive, as you've surely read as well."

As Longarm dove into the chili con carne Concho nodded soberly and said, "You don't talk like a Canadian. You talk more like that West Virginian you claim to be, no offense. Pues . . . no se. Este comida apesta, no?"

Without thinking, Longarm replied, "Pero no, es muy buena!" in all sincerity, because the food wasn't bad at all and he'd started out the evening hungry as a bitch wolf with no supper.

So Concho nodded gravely and decided, "No tengo razón, lo se, pero my people tell tales of a tall gringo lawman who has much of West Virginia in his English and a little of Chihuahua in his Spanish. They call him El Brazo Largo. More importantly, they say this gringo has ridden through the Sierra Madres, more than once, without losing his pitón y huevos to Los Yaquis."

Longarm washed down a wad of tortilla with the cheap coffee and just waited. He figured Concho would tell him if there was any point to all this pussyfooting.

Concho did. "Bueno, I have perhaps sixty whole dollars coming to me from the company, if it ever gets here. After that I had made no plans at all because old Pink only hired a greaser to tell him what some of the help were really saying about a boss who has to start drinking before noon."

Longarm asked cautiously, "Are you asking if I'd like to make it worth your while to get word to my home office?"

Concho shook his head. "I just sent Bunny up the Butterfield spur to check your tale of woe. If you're really who you say you are, Pink Atwell ain't about to let you out of here alive.

Would *you* want to own up to a comical mistake like that if you were already sort of famous for screwing up drunk?"

Longarm gulped and declared, "You'd never get away with it, old son. Once he'd verified I got as far as Shakespeare, my boss would never rest till he found out where I'd wound up, see?"

Concho said, "*I* see. Pink Atwell may figure some of our flooded mine shafts do hide a lot of foolish mistakes. Meanwhile, there's this high-toned hidalgo lady staying over to the hotel. She's been trying to hire someone to carry her on down to her daddy's hacienda in the foothills of the Sierra Madre. She says it would be worth at least five hundred dollars, Yanqui, to her dear old daddy. I got the gun. I got the nerve, and I sure could used the money. But I had to say no, when she asked sort of desperate the other night, because I just don't have the know-how to get a pretty lady and her hired help through Yaqui country. How do you like my offer so far?"

Longarm washed down some chili, burped, and decided, "You made more sense when you said no. We'd be talking a mighty long ride if this hacienda the lady needs to get to lies south of Yaqui country. It could hardly lie *in* Yaqui country, so just how far down into a country I ain't supposed to visit might we have under consideration?"

Concho took a thoughtful drag on his smoke. "She did mention something about a trail over the mountains between Casas Grandes and Nacezan in Sonora. Did I forget to tell you I wanted *all* that five hundred as my share? I figure getting you out of a fix like this, at the cost of my job and back pay, ought to satisfy any honest man such as the real Brazo Largo."

Longarm smiled thinly and growled, "If you thought I was anybody else you wouldn't even consider riding into Yaqui country with me. I know the parts of the Sierra Madre the lady mentioned. It ain't on the far side of Yaqui country. It's smack in the middle of a stretch the Mexican army only passes through backed by field artillery and keeping to the few mapped trails."

He sipped more coffee as he considered others he knew who raised beef where others might fear to tread. He decided, "Well, the Jingle Bob lets the Apache help themselves to an occasional side of beef in exchange for a live-and-let-live attitude toward its riders. I know a pretty lady over Texas way who calls a Comanche chief her honorary uncle and they don't even rape her heifers. So tell me more about this sweet señorita who needs a guide through Yaqui country if her daddy gets along with 'em that well."

Concho shook his head. "First you say yes. Then all five of us get the hell out of here before sunrise and all hell to pay. She'll doubtless be proud to tell you her whole tale of woe about a gringo husband who beat her as we carry her on home. But unless we're well south of the border before Pink Atwell sees we're gone . . ."

So Longarm set what was left of his supper aside and got to his feet, saying, "Bueno, Vámonos pa'l carajo."

But Concho insisted, "I have your word as an hombre? You won't just tell us to screw ourselves once you're out of here, with your guns, your possibles, and your riding stock back?"

Longarm held out his hand to shake on it, saying, "I'd have to see all the ladies concerned before I'd suggest any screwing. I give you my word I won't double-cross *you,* though. So when do we start for Yaqui country and doubtless a gruesome death?"

Concho said, "Douse that lantern," as he unlocked the big iron door. So Longarm did, resisting the impulse to mention that poor Mex he'd had to kill, as an act of mercy, after finding him a mite worked over by Yaqui in the Sierra Madres.

Once they were out in the dark, Concho led the way up the slope until Longarm figured they could be most anywhere. Then they entered an abandoned shack. Concho said it had been the shack of a laid-off miner and his family as he lit another lamp inside, adding, "The rest of your belongings are still where you left 'em in that tack room at the livery. I'll fetch 'em, along with your stock, when I pick up those others at the hotel."

As Longarm moved over to the kitchen table, where his wallet, guns, and all had been waiting for him, Concho said, "Don't open the heavy window drapes. Should anyone knock on the door, don't open it because it won't be me. I got the key, and nobody else ought to care whether anyone's home or not."

Longarm said he'd sit quiet as a church mouse. So Concho left and locked the door after him as Longarm filled his pockets and strapped on his good old .44-40 again.

Since Longarm was human, the next thoughts that crossed his mind were only natural. But aside from having given his word, there were practical reasons to make a man reconsider a double cross.

Aside from the dangers of meeting up with an understandably pissed-off Concho in or about the livery before he could mount up and ride out, the long night ride back to Shakespeare only sounded like a dash for safety till one considered confederates of Shadowy Saunders who'd know him on sight better than vice versa. They'd have surely told him at the Western Union if anyone in Denver had wired direct orders to get a paid-up lawman killed as a wanted outlaw. So the slithering sons of bitches had to be using some code, if not a set of prepared plans to be followed according to most any sort of pre-set signal, from an innocent birthday greeting to no wire at all. Longarm had read somewhere about ways to shut off dangerous machinery in some steam plants just by not resetting some clockwork now and again. He was able to come up with many a way to signal unseen confederates at a distance, and he doubted he spent as much time dreaming up dirty tricks as Shadowy Saunders, the sickly son of a bitch!

So Longarm had made up his mind to go along with Concho and those other suicidal maniacs by the time the door popped open without any warning and Concho ducked back in with two other natural Mexicans and a sort of Greek goddess carved out of ivory and burnished bronze. Her flat Spanish hat and charro-cut riding habit were the same shade of coppery brown. A gal needed mucho dinero, if not dye-mixing skills, to rate duds that harmonized so closely with her pinned-up hair. Her big doe eyes were a more penny-bright shade of copper as they were introduced by Concho. Her full name was Desdemona followed by a one of those firecracker strings of names that went with Spanish folks of quality. As she shook hands with him democratically, she said it was jake with her if he called her Mona, seeing they'd be sharing the hazards of a dangerous game on the trail south.

He smiled thinly and replied, "For openers, Miss Mona, I never follow trails in Yaqui country. Yaqui lurk along trails a lot like cats lurk along baseboards. A smart mouse tries not to follow the usual customs of his kind when he knows for certain he's up against really good cats. But before I lay out the basic moves of a dangerous game indeed, are you dead certain you can't be persuaded to get home some other way?"

The pallid copper-haired Spanish lady sighed and said, "There *is* no other way. No safer way, at any rate. It is too long a story to go into now, but suffice it to say certain people of your kind, in the pay of my late husband's family, are already searching for me on this side of the border. I fear they may have wired bad things about me to the Mexican authorities. You know how our so-called law-and-order government in Ciudad Mejico plays toady to outsiders with any political pull."

Longarm grimaced and said, "I surely do. I don't have such pull and Los Rurales have tried to blow holes in me more than once. I'd still rather run into them than Yaqui in the Sierra Madres, though."

Mona quietly said, "That's because you could not know any Yaqui as well as my family and I. We have been ranching on the east slope of the Sierra Madre for three generations now. Contrary to all you may have heard, the Yaqui are simply untamed savages, not lunatics. You see, during a severe drought, at a time a great comet was seen above the burning chaparral of the Sierra Madre, my great grandfather, Don Diego Hernan, came across this Yaqui woman and seven

116

children, dying of thirst by a dried-out water hole. So . . ."

"I've heard much the same tale, involving Comanche and such," Longarm said. "Some Indians can be like that. As far back as the French and Indians Wars some white families out in the pines tended to be spared by warriors capable of utter savagery, along with gratitude for long-remembered favors. But what do you need with old Concho and me if you and your'n are on such good terms with the only Quill Indians in the Sierra Madres this far north?"

She demurely replied, "I have no reason to fear any *Indians*. It is Los Rurales y Los Federales I do not wish to meet in the Sierra Madre or anywhere else. As you must surely know, both the mounted police and our roughneck cavalry are out in force, all along the border, trying to round up your own sweet Apache in cooperation with the U.S. Army."

Pointing her riding crop at the slightly older and far plumper Mestizo gal who'd come in with her, Mona explained, as if she needed to, "The animals our glorious El Presidente sends out on horseback to protect us from one another would not hesitate to abuse my Lucia here, and she is not wanted by the law on either side of the border!"

The already dusky Lucia blushed a becoming shade of damask rose. All over. It was easy to tell because, being a servant, Lucia wore a pleated white cotton skirt and a matching low-cut blouse. The old manservant closer to the door was dressed more charro, although his bolero jacket and bell-bottom pants were plain gray wool and his big sombrero was unbleached straw.

None of that concerned Longarm as much as what their boss lady had just said about the law. As a lawman, Longarm felt obliged to speak up. "Hold on, ma'am. Were you just saying you were wanted here in the States for some statutory offense?"

She lowered her thick lashes to confess, "Just a little one. As the result of a domestic dispute. Señor Morales tells us you are a federal marshal with reasons of your own for slipping south of the border, no?"

Longarm had been wondering what Concho's real name might be. He smiled thinly at the young Mex as he told the lady, "Close enough. Before I go aiding and abetting, ma'am, I'd like to hear more about your reasons for heading home to Old Mexico so sudden."

But before she could answer her old manservant suddenly blurted out, in Spanish, "This is madness. Is true the patróna may be known to those Yaqui we are certain to meet, despite this gringo's idle boasting about gringo mice! Is true Lucia and I may get by as your servants, despite our being member of another Indio race they hate as much as they hate other outsiders. But they will never accept a third Mejicano and this outright *extranjero*!"

There was no way to translate "extranjero" with the acid bile in the old peon's tone. "Stranger" was only the official meaning. He doubtless meant it the way Irish Papists meant that verse in the song that went:

> As I go walking down the street,
> The people from their doorsteps blather,
> There goes that Protestant son of a bitch!
> The one who shagged O'Riley's daughter!

Mona said soothingly, "Let me worry about our Yaqui friends, Pepillo. We need these caballeros to help us avoid those far more dangerous military patrols. The Yaqui won't hurt us. You'll see."

The old cuss shook his big straw sombrero stubbornly and told her, "No, I won't. I quit. I like it better up this way to begin with, and nothing anyone can say or do will ever persuade me I wish for to die as those Yaqui can make one die, a thousand times over, before they finally finish!"

Then he was out the door, even as Mona called, "Come back here, Pepillo! Where do you think you are going?"

Concho went after him, shouting back, "I'll stop him. The rest of you had better get aboard those ponies tethered out back."

Then he was gone as Mona told Longarm, "We brought your mount and pack mule from the livery, along with our own. Why don't we put out that light and do as he just suggested?"

Longarm couldn't think of a smarter move at the moment. So a few moments later he and the two gals were out in the fenced-in backyard with the nine saddled or packsaddled brutes Concho had been talking about.

Longarm was pleased to see his Winchester was still in the boot of his old McClellan. He figured on going through his saddlebags later. He doubted any sneak thief would pass up a saddle gun to steal an old tweed suit, shaving soap, and such. The plump Lucia got up on her mule sidesaddle. Mona forked herself astride aboard a barb pony. That was the first time Longarm noticed her innocent-looking pleated skirts were split for such mannish riding. He knew it might help, with such rough riding likely ahead.

He swung up on his army gelding last, to be polite, just before Concho rejoined them alone. Concho said, "We'd better move it on out. We'll need all the pack brutes, but we may as well leave that one saddle mule where it is."

Mona said, "I'm sure he'll come to his senses any minute, and I'd hate to leave such an old family retainer behind."

Concho insisted, swinging up into his own saddle, "I don't want to be here if he comes back with company! Pink Atwell was talking earlier about dropping Deputy Long down mine shafts, and I don't know how I'd ever explain a prisoner aboard a pony with his guns back on. So, coño, no me friegues y *vámonos*!"

Longarm didn't argue with Concho either as the four of them moved out the gate at a walk, leading the four pack brutes. Mona was a good sport about that, with one servant less.

They naturally rode sedately, along a contour line up the slope from the main street, till they were well clear of Chrysolite and Concho pointed down to the west in the moonlight, saying there was a trail at least as far as the border down on the flats.

Longarm told Concho, "Anyone watching for a border jump would have that trail staked out. We'll ride safer, and likely not much slower, up here amid the higher chaparral."

Concho asked who might be out to head them off this early. He said, "I don't see how Pink and the boys could be missing any of us this early."

Longarm started to ask a dumb question. But he decided a killing he didn't know about for certain might not be federal, and surely ought to be able to wait until he had old Concho back on his own side of the border again. He said, "No telling who might be staked out where, with two armies hunting Indians and at least one outlaw gang hunting *me*."

So they rode on, and on some more, changing mounts around two in the morning, until the moon was way low to the west and the sky was getting light enough to the east to make out the inky raggedy crest line of the Hatchet Range, known this far south as the Sierra Hachita.

They'd been riding over scree the structure and sound of knapped gun flints for some time when Concho, in the lead, called back to swing down-slope, explaining, "Cholla ahead. A real jungle of cactus the devil must have made when God wasn't looking!"

Longarm called back, "Hold on, old son. Is it creeping cholla or jumping cholla?"

The seasoned Mex rider snorted, "Jumping, of course. Why did you think I was so anxious to avoid it?"

Longarm laughed and announced, "This must be the place, as the prophet said."

Then he reined in, adding, "We'd all best dismount and do this with some delicacy. The moon's still bright enough. But the nasty pincushions do seem to jump right through the air at you if you even brush a hooked spine with a loose sleeve. We'd best lead the stock in carefully one at a time."

Mona surprised him by asking what on earth he was talking about. "Nobody in their right mind would want to lead a pony into a thick growth of jumping cholla! Why would they want to get anywhere near it themselves?"

He chuckled and explained, "You just answered your own question. We've likely made it this far somewhere south of the border unobserved. I want us to *stay* unobserved through the daylight hours by day-camping in this swell cactus patch nobody with a lick of sense would have any other call to ride anywhere near."

She laughed like a mean little kid and told him she could see, now, why the peones said neither bandidos nor Los Rurales would ever kill El Brazo Largo.

He warned her not to talk childish as he dismounted, and added, "If you'd be kind enough to hold these reins for me, I mean to see if there's any way in at all. Meanwhile, the only sure way to avoid the mean gents you grow down here amid all your cactus is by simply staying north of the infernal border!"

Leaving her with that thought, Longarm and his Winchester went exploring afoot in the moonlight. The Winchester was meant more for the jumping cholla than anything he expected to jump out of it at him.

Jumping cholla was a variety of opuntia that grew up to two or three stories tall in a sort of apple-tree shape. But it was much meaner. Where a sensible small tree or big bush had leaves, the cholla had all these greenish white fuzz balls armed with the most vicious cactus spines ever invented by Professor Darwin. Each hair-thin but up to three-inch-long needle was barbed, like a porcupine quill. So you only had to be hooked by one for the whole damned pad, the size and weight of a crab apple, to bust loose from its branch and sort of jump all over you, driving spine after spine in as it rolled on down, leaving each and every spine stuck where it had dug in.

But as Longarm had hoped, this hillside grove of jumping cholla had flourished about fifteen feet high, to form its thorny canopy well above the rough barked trunks, each standing six or eight feet away from one another.

The stony ground was clearer than one might expect from outside such a tangle. Cactus wrens and pack rats gathered the spines up as they fell, this time of the year, for the nests they somehow managed to make out of such wicked shit. The shade from above, along with the dew that tended to settle at night on the scree, had encouraged less vicious growth, mostly tarweed and rabbit bush, to flourish amid the cholla trunks as a handy ground-level screen against casual eyes from further up or down the slope. So once he'd busted off some of the lower cholla branches with his steel gun barrel, Longarm went back out to announce, "Just about perfect for a daytime hideout. No water to attract unwelcome visitors, which is why we're packing all those water bags. There's room to tether our stock, and the scree won't be too rough to stretch out on once we spread some brush and our ground tarps over it. So let's get cracking. Concho, you and me had best lead the stock in, a head at a time, while the ladies make camp as far in as it goes before you commence coming out the other side."

Nobody argued. So in less than half an hour they were set up deep in the cholla about as snug as your average bug in any rug had any right to feel.

Having warned the two women any campfire would be out of the question, Longarm was more puzzled than surprised to find Mona and her maidservant had set up sort of separate camps, screened from one another by lots of rabbit bush and even some needle grass. He wasn't dumb enough to ask why his own packsaddle and such were in the same clearing with Mona's unrolled bedding. He just unsaddled his mount and unrolled his own ground cloth atop the springy rabbit bush someone had been considerate enough to spread right next to her own.

They'd timed it about right. They could see one another better now as they lounged side by side at the break of day. Naturally they were still fully dressed atop their bedding. She'd already asked and he'd already explained they'd have to wait a spell to find out just how much shade or breeze they were likely to rate up here above the regular trail south. She'd said she wasn't tired enough to turn in anyway.

He'd have thought her greener to these parts had she not busted off some rabbit bush twigs to chew. That encouraged him to buy her tale about being raised on a hacienda down this way, in spite of her cameo features and high-toned English. For few strangers to the dry Southwest would be likely to take up such habits on their own. White kids generally needed Indian playmates to introduce them to chewing rabbit bush. The aromatic shrubbery smelled like medicine a strict mamma might force on you. But the rubbery sap did chew just like that candy-store gum once all the sugar had been chewed out.

Longarm helped himself to some, in lieu of a more expensive morning smoke, as he faced her cross-legged and said, "Well, so far so good, and at this rate we ought to see you safely home in no more than a few night rides like that last one."

Then he tried, "Seeing we're south of the border now, where my writ as a lawman don't run, would you like to tell me why that husband you left has someone else after you?"

She laid her hat aside and let down her long copper coils with a relieved toss of her head as she announced, "I was never afraid of Walter when he was alive!"

Then she proceeded to tell Longarm more than he'd ever wanted to know about a proud Spanish beauty meeting up with a spoiled rich kid while attending college out San Francisco way. Longarm had been wondering where she'd learned to talk so American in a sort of la-di-da way. He said gently, "Lots of young college gals away from home meet up with sweet talkers they might feel a mite sorry about later. You say this Walter you wed is no longer with us, Miss Mona?"

She nodded. "He *knew* I was a Coronado Lopez Vargas y Vasquez, and yet he actually raised a hand to me when I chided him about molesting my Lucia while he was drunk and I was . . . indisposed."

Longarm nodded soberly. "Some drunks are like that. I hope he didn't really hit you, ma'am?"

She sniffed. "Of course not. I shot him right between the eyes when he said he was going to and actually took two steps toward me with his hand raised as if to strike!"

Longarm gulped, sighed, and muttered, "Why me, Lord? Might you have real lawmen after you with a murder warrant, Miss Mona?"

She shook her head, insisting, "I never murdered anyone. I shot an unfeeling brute who trifled with the servants and tried to *frighten* me. I don't see how anyone could call that a crime!"

To which he could only reply, "It's easy, ma'am. You just call the law and tell 'em somebody's been murdered. I take it you and your servants decamped shorty before or after your late husband's body might have been noticed by anyone else?"

She nodded, explaining, "We were staying at his parents' home on Nob Hill at the time. So I imagine they found Walter dead when they returned from a trip to Sacramento. I left them a polite note but, as you suggested, they did seem to want to press charges. When I read about it in the Tucson papers I thought we'd better return to my own parents more discreetly, and the rest you know."

Longarm grinned crookedly and muttered, "I do indeed, and I'm sure glad I didn't know earlier, even though it don't sound like a federal case. I ain't supposed to aid and abet fleeing felons, no offense, but seeing you've already made it to Old Mexico, where they seem to understand such family disputes better, we'll just say no more about it till we see you safely home, Lord willing and neither the Indians nor the soldiers hunting 'em slaughter the whole bunch of us."

Chapter 14

Knowing snakes, scorpions, and other such menaces of this cactus country started searching for shade within the hour after sunrise, Longarm told Mona to just sit tight and chew her rabbit bush while he made an inspection.

Packing his Winchester at port arms, he moved out to the shady edge of their cholla thicket for a study of their open surroundings. It was already getting warmer, even in the shade, but he'd left his denim work jacket on. Nobody but a total asshole wanted to walk through jumping cholla in his shirtsleeves.

He only picked up a dozen or so murderous spines, none of them all the way through his hat or sleeves, as he made a complete circuit of their eight or ten acres of discouraging shit. Along the sunnier edges the cholla branches spread further out from the main trunks, to bend over and dangle their hellish fuzz balls within a yard or so of the stony ground. Their shade encouraged the sprouting of needle grass, poppies, sotol, and that ubiquitous rabbit bush.

Farther out, in every direction, you saw more blooming greasewood than anything else. Greasewood never grew too close to other desert growth and vice versa. The Indians held its roots had big medicine that held back other thirsty roots in a land the thunderbird didn't seem too interested in.

At the moment, Longarm thought it more important that any riders or even dismounted desert rovers within miles would be visible as hell within miles coming through such low chaparral. Anybody as low-slung as, say, a coyote or a crawling man could doubtless work in a lot closer, provided he had any sensible motive for doing so.

Glancing the other way, Longarm couldn't see more than a dozen or so yards deep into the cholla, and it was *jumping* cholla.

Once he'd circled to where they'd first entered the nasty shit, and saw they hadn't left any horse turds on the flinty scree as a sign to follow, he nodded at the shimmering far horizon and told it, "You go on and bake all you like out yonder. Nobody but army officers would be dumb enough to travel about now, and even they would want to follow that distant trail I can just make out from up this way."

Then he ducked under some low-hanging cholla to more or less follow the same route in as he'd found earlier in the dark. But he had no call to retrace his footsteps to the inch, and so he was off by maybe a few yards when he heard girlish giggles from the far side of some chest-high brush and eased over for a look-see over the pretty flowers.

Considering how romantic it felt, fucking dog-style on a bedroll sure looked silly when somebody else was at it, all hot and sweaty. So Longarm crawfished politely back before Concho or the little Mestiza maidservant, Lucia, caught him peeking at them.

He was still smiling wistfully—that Lucia had a great little ass—as he rejoined the lady Lucia worked for in their own shady clearing. He hadn't noticed in the earlier light how prettily the knee-high spears of bluebonnet had blossomed in the dappled shade.

You couldn't tell from his side of her covers, but Mona had to be wearing less in her bedroll than the coppery riding habit she'd hung neatly to air over some brush. She was wide awake, reclining under just a cotton sheet, as he put down his Winchester and took off his jacket with care, saying, "The

126

most dangerous things within miles would seem to be the fuzz balls screening us from the sun at the moment. But I'll stay awake so the rest of you can catch some sleep."

"Your friend, Señor Morales, has been abusing my Lucia!" she suddenly cried, as if he was supposed to do something about it.

He nodded soberly and replied, "I noticed they seemed on friendly terms, ma'am. It wasn't too clear who might be abusing whom. Nobody was yelling for help. So ain't it barely possible old Lucia sort of enjoys such abuse, as you call it?"

She almost sobbed. "That's what Walter tried to use as an excuse! You men are all alike! I wouldn't be surprised to see you rutting like an animal with my Mestiza servant!"

Longarm calmly plucked a cholla spine from the jacket atop his raised knee, as he kept his distance on his own bedding and replied, "I reckon Concho would be surprised. He saw her first."

Mona smiled despite herself and said, "He did indeed! Without a stitch! So what are we going to do about it?"

Longarm got rid of another cholla spine and observed, "Concho don't work for me. I ain't sure this would be a good time for you to fire either one of 'em, ma'am. Telling folks not to fornicate, once they've got into each other's forbidden fruit, strikes me as an exercise in futility. It's dumb to lay down laws you can't enforce. Ben Franklin tried to explain that to his pals in London that time and . . . Mayhaps, in your case, the Spanish Inquisition would be a better illustration. It just ain't possible to prevent a tolerable amount of sinning, Miss Mona. It's tough enough to prevent such sins as highway robbery. That's why I got to get you home, swing north, and get back to Chrysolite with some backing, before that mining company sends in its last big payroll."

She rolled over on her other side, exposing some bare back to him as she started to sniffle. He knew better than to say a word to any gal who did that. If a man asked what was wrong they'd be sure to tell him and, damn it, he'd never done shit to either her or her lusty Lucia, damn old Concho's eyes.

So he'd gotten all the cactus spines out of his jacket and hat by the time Mona suddenly blurted out, "Don't you find me as attractive as my Indian maidservant, ah, Custis?"

Longarm went on unbuckling his gun rig as he quietly replied, "That'd be like comparing apples and prickly pear fruit, ma'am. You're both handsome women, each in her own way. If you're asking whether I'd rather fuck you than her, I reckon it would depend."

She gasped, and he could see by her exposed spine that she blushed mighty rosy under that pale ivory hide. She took a deep breath before she said, "Did you have to word that so crudely?"

He set his .44-40 and rolled-up gunbelt by the Winchester at the head end of his roll as he calmly replied, "It was you wanting to know, ma'am. When you cut through all the courtly bull, all you females really want to know is whether us men want to fuck you or somebody else. I know it's supposed to be a big secret. I still say the day Queen Victoria met Prince Albert at the altar they both knew he was going to wind up fucking her in the mighty near future, and judging from all the kids they had, he must have."

She laughed despite herself, then sobered and insisted, "A true caballero is still supposed to express his desires in more delicate terms when he pays court to a maiden."

Longarm started to unbutton his shirt as he pointed out, "I ain't no caballero. I ain't courting you, and if you're still a maiden I can see why your late husband was fooling around with the hired help!"

She sobbed. "That's a vicious thing to even imply! I'll have you know no man has ever complained about me in bed!"

He resisted the temptation. She'd already told him she'd shot her husband *outside* the covers, and that reference to men in the plural sense hinted at other little secrets she hadn't gotten to yet. But he knew she would, if he didn't get her on home soon. So he cast his shirt aside and reclined atop the covers, lighting a morning cheroot now that the flare of a match would hardly catch anyone's eye from out on the shimmering desert.

Mona left him in peace for a time. Then she rolled back over to face him, her pretty little face framed by all that coppery unbound hair, as she asked him if he could spare her a cheroot.

He nodded and tossed a cheroot and the tin of waterproof Mex matches her way. The matches fell a mite short. A mite too short for her modesty, he saw, as she groped out from under her sheet in vain, despite the grand view of her bare arm, shoulder, and doubtless more of that one tit than she figured he could see from his modest distance.

He sighed and crawled over to pick up the damned matches and light the damned cheroot between her pouty lips. She placed one soft hand on his tanner wrist to steady the flame, no matter how unsteady it might make a man feel. But he'd been teased by meaner-hearted professionals with more sinister motives. So he just kept a poker face till she was properly lit, then shook out the match and straightened up to return to his own bedding. As he turned his back on her she muttered a really dreadful thing in Spanish. He turned to face her, hunkered on his hams, as he calmly replied, "My mother was married to my father a decent interval before my date of birth, ma'am. As for me preferring the asshole of a choirboy to the cunt of a grown woman, that's for me to know and you to find out, if you'd care to ask nicer."

She blushed so red he feared for her health as he said, "I reckon you didn't know a gringo would know what funciete meant. It being such an obscure obscenity to high-class Mexicans. I reckon I should have warned you I learned such Border Mex as I know from a less refined crowd than you usually run with."

She laughed weakly and confessed, "One hears one's servants in their quarters, living in El Norte where even the walls of grander homes are so thin. Where are you going, Custis?"

He said, "Back to my own bedding. I doubt there's a choirboy within miles."

She lowered her lashes to murmur, "I understand. Walter said I reminded him of a marble stature with no feelings too.

But I did not shoot him for neglecting me. Maybe I did not mind his neglecting me, once he started coming to bed drunk. But he should have been a little more discreet, and he certainly shouldn't have raised a hand to a lady!"

Longarm said, "I'm sure he was mighty sorry just as that gun went off in his face, ma'am. Up until then, he was likely a mite confused by your conflicting signals."

She demanded, "What do you mean? What you just said about that queen and her consort was perfectly true, in its own crude way. Walter was allowed to . . . how does one put it?"

"Chingar?" he suggested, inspiring her to cough on her smoke.

"Hacer el amor would be putting it crudely enough," she said. "I would never come right out and say such a vile word, even to my husband, even while he was doing it to me!"

Longarm nodded. "That doubtless explains what he was doing with pretty little Lucia then. You gals are right about us menfolk being more uncouth. More uncouth than most of you, leastways. But if you'd like some advice from a pal, next time you wind up making amor with some horny cuss, tell him you'd just love for him to venir in your furioso."

She tossed the hardly used cheroot on the flinty dirt between them and rolled over again, sobbing that she wasn't used to being spoken to that way, even by a lover.

He grunted, "That's all right. I ain't your lover and I have to *pay* for them damned cheroots, you spoiled sass."

He moved closer to pick up the barely smoked cheroot as she stiffened her bare spine and warned, "Don't you dare try to kiss me, you brute!"

He laughed, not unkindly, and started to turn away again. But she rolled back over, not even trying to cover her cherry-nippled vanilla cupcakes as she almost wailed, "Why are you teasing me this way, Custis? I'm *not* a frigid bitch with an ice pack between her marble thighs! I'm *not*! I'm *not*!"

So Longarm moved back to take the poor trembling thing in his own bare arms and assure her he felt sure she was "nada más sube el culo." Which inspired her to laugh weakly, say that calling her an easy piece of ass might be putting it a bit strong, and then drag him under the sheet with her as if to prove him right.

It wasn't that simple. She was naked as a jay under that thin cotton. But he still had his boots and jeans on. Worse yet, he'd left his guns an unsafe distance from her. So once he'd kissed her deep and fingered her shallow to prove she meant it, he whipped over to his own bedding and got back to her, with his Winchester, before she could jerk off all the way.

Seeing he'd inspired her that much with all their earlier pussy-footing, he just unbuttoned his fly to haul out his fully charged organ-grinder and thrust it deep in her passion-slicked crotch as she went right on playing with her engorged clit, eyes shut, teeth clenched, and moaning deep in her pretty chest like a she-wolf in heat until, just as he was getting started, her big penny-bright eyed opened wide and she gasped, "Madre de Dios! What are you *doing* to me, señor?"

He said he thought it was obvious. But as he worked his pants down without stopping Mona marveled, "Pero no, my husband, I confess, was not the only man I ever . . . did *that* with. This is not the same. Look, I can enjoy it without fingering myself at all and, oh, Custis, *chingé* me! Chingé me mucho!"

So he did. She really liked it when he braced an elbow under each of her knees to spread her wider and plumb her deeper, she said, than any man had ever managed before.

She was likely telling the truth. Her firm young torso was a mite longer than most. So her vagina, while sweetly tight by nature or on purpose, seemed a mite deeper than average. Lots of gals in the past had complained about the length of Longarm's shaft, once he had them really spread on a firm surface, but old Mona said it felt like the vera chingadera young girls dream about, playing with themselves in the shit-house, just like young boys.

Having established they both enjoyed real fucking, Longarm got rid of his pants and boots to start over in a position she sobbed was just too uncouth, even as she arched her spine to

131

take another uncouth inch, although she refused to let him cast their sheet to the winds and really play Adam and Eve in the Garden.

And so, what with one uncouth position and another, the morning passed all too soon. They took turns staying awake and on guard once it got too hot, even in the shade, to do anything better.

Then the setting sun was painting the sky rosy and gilding the cactus spines above to resemble shredded telegraph wire. So Longarm and Mona were dressed when they were joined by Concho and a bashfully smiling Lucia, who sheepishly asked if anyone expected her to cook supper.

Longarm said warm meals were out for now, and explained he'd loaded up on grub one could eat cold with that very plan in mind.

Even though the three of them were more used to gringo grub than your average Mex, it was still sort of comical to hear Boston baked beans, cheddar cheese, and plain old soda crackers complimented as mighty fine, if somewhat exotic, trail grub.

He'd filled his saddle canteens back in Shakespeare with good stiff coffee, brewed so strong you could dilute it by more than half with bag water and it would still jar you awake drunk cold.

They took their time, and let the snakes settle down from their sunset hunting before they saddled up. So the open desert lay black as a politician's promise under the blazing stars and quarter moon as they forged on south, trending ever higher and to their east, till Concho asked how come, adding, "Ain't we likely to meet more Yaqui in tall timber than out on the open desert this time of the year?"

Longarm said, "Yep, but not as many this far north, as if we have the whole blamed Continental Divide to cross, where the high Sierra Madres climb high as our own Rockies, smack in the middle of Yaqui country. Miss Mona's home spread lies on the east slope of the main ridge. Meanwhile, I recall a pass way lower, where the Hatchets commence to climb aboard the Sierra Madres. It's an outlaw pass. Some friendly outlaws showed me over it while I was working on some Mexican free enterprise involving Texas cattle winding up on that newer Arizona range."

Hoping he knew what he was talking about, he continued. "I'm betting on neither the Yaqui nor the soldiers hunting 'em would be using such a pass too often. Cattle thieves sort of like to travel alone."

Mona, who'd been listening from his other side, protested that she was still more worried about running into rurales or federales than Indians her family still fed now and again.

Longarm sighed and said, "I'd be fibbing if I said I'd rather be captured by Yaqui than Los Rurales. But not all that much. Last I heard, some infernal Mex governor had put out another bounty on me, dead or alive, and you know how lazy them rurales can be with a prisoner when taking him in alive just doesn't matter."

Chapter 15

They holed up the next day atop a wind-swept mesa surrounded on most sides by sheer cliffs and shaded from the unfriendly sun by tangle-trunked juniper, the feather branches almost meeting a good twelve feet up.

When Lucia, being more Indian, complained there were no piñons, Longarm explained, "I recalled this hole in the sky with just such matters in mind, Lucia. There's no water up here either. So why would anyone else bother coming all the way up here by broad day when there's nothing worth gathering but indifferent firewood?"

Concho opined juniper poles didn't even make good fencing, that Yaqui strung no wire fencing to begin with, and that he'd known what he was doing when he recruited a man who'd survived in Yaqui country before.

Then he took Lucia by one hand and led her off somewhere. Mona said she doubted they were interested in gathering juniper berries. She laughed when Longarm pointed out it was downright impossible to gather anything that was not in season, adding, "You can hunt for piñon nuts at any time where piñons grow. The ground squirrels and pack rats gather 'em in considerable caches amid the rocks if you're really that interested in piñon nuts. I doubt even a Paiute digger would expect to find any up this way."

She suggested they search for a private spot to enjoy more vera chingadera. So they did. Old Mona had sure gotten earthy since he'd proven she wasn't packing an ice bag between her more muscular than marble thighs. She'd hauled him off in the dark, during a trail break the night before, to do a quick one in her riding habit. It hadn't been easy standing up, thanks to that split skirt not being as loose as she'd thought.

That morning on the mesa was far nicer. She called it, "El rapto supremo!" as they did it stripped down all the way in an improvised tent she invented with a sheet and some cooperative little trees.

Later, somewhere in the dark, they must have made it over the outlaw pass he'd been aiming for by the stars. There were just two sorts of passes over a serious divide. Fortunately, the main spine of North America is old enough, and complex enough, to offer both the narrow natural-ambush variety and many a broader and lower stretch of mountain scenery where a greenhorn could hardly tell if he was on one side of the divide or the other until he came to some running stream.

Longarm and his companions came to one, running east toward the even broader Chihuahua Desert, just in time to refill all the water bags before they holed up again in a hundred-acre prickly pear flat, where the shade was provided more by tarps and sheeting draped across those flowering and hence fruitless cactus pads nobody else had call to care about.

That afternoon, scouting the perimeter of their cactus patch, Longarm spotted smoke signals on higher ground off to their west. Mona calmly decided they'd been spotted by Yaqui, but didn't seem worried about it.

As they ate supper Longarm thought back to every move they'd made getting this far. Then he decided, "It ain't us that smoke talk is describing. Indians are good, damned good, on their own ground. But they ain't mind readers and they don't read sign where no sign's been left for 'em to read."

Concho said, "There's always some sign. And you are only human too, you know."

Longarm shook his head. "There's no modest way to say it. So let's just say I've been hunted in the past by Indians who knew for certain I was about. If I'd been caught we wouldn't be having this discussion about my pussy-footing skills. We never got the chance to wire any Yaqui we were coming. I've been leading us across a lot of scree and slick-rock. Such hoofprints and horse apples as we'd had to leave behind shouldn't add up much to any Yaqui scout who had no call to scout for us to begin with. So how do you like a less cautious party, doubtless way bigger, attracting all them smoky comments as they've been moving by broad day, Lord knows how close?"

Mona started to get up, sobbing something about her honor. But Longarm hauled her back down, saying, "They ain't *that* close. I just now scouted all around. The smoke-talker over to our west can doubtless see way farther out across the flats to the east. I'll bet that even as we speak some federale column is fixing to make camp for the night after a long dusty day on the trail. So we'll just give them and the snakes time to settle in for the night and—"

"How do you know they're not those dreadful rurales?" Mona asked.

So he explained. "Rurales ride in smaller bunches, and blend in with local customs way more than old boys inducted out of the slums of Ciudad Mejico. Rurales in Yaqui country would be moving as cautious as us. Mayhaps more so. I doubt any of their kith and kin have even done any Yaqui any favors."

He reached for one of his last smokes as he told her, "Either way, we ought to have you safely home in a night's ride or so. I reckon we'd best try for sooner rather than later. We're back on fairly open range, those other riders make me feel proddy, and I got way more serious riding ahead if I'm to work my way back north of the border, round up a posse, and tame that damned mining town before those outlaws get around to it!"

As he glanced up at the slight light purple sky, Mona placed a thoughtful palm on his denim-clad thigh, murmuring, "I do not see how I could have gotten home any faster. These nights, and days, on the trail with you have passed so swiftly. I don't suppose you would like to spend a little time, perhaps a month, on my family hacienda once we safely get there?"

He blew a wistful smoke ring and softly replied, "I reckon I'd like it way better than your family, querida mia. You're surely going to have a lot of catching up to do with your kin, and your dear old dad will doubtless want you to talk to a good Mex lawyer as well. I'd only be in the way, even if I had the time and hadn't learned a thing or two about, well, ships that pass in the night."

She asked, in a hurt tone, if she meant no more to him than a ship he'd passed in the night.

He said gently, "Hell, *I* ain't nothing but a ship neither. What I mean was that nothing lasts forever. Queen Victoria would be the first to tell you the grandest love story has to end in a tragedy, unless it ends in a bedroom farce. I've sometimes thought a romance cut short through neither side's fault, while all the flowers were still sweetly blooming, might not make for the best of memories later on, when the one you got stuck with burns supper and gets to nagging some more about that more ambitious rascal she should have married up with instead."

She got up and wandered off in the cactus to take a leak, cry, or whatever. He'd had the same conversation with grown men who'd failed to follow his drift. He'd caught himself choking up more than once over gals like good old Roping Sally, up Montana way, who'd wound up dead before he'd worn out all the nice things to say to them and before they'd started nagging him about getting his fool self a decent job.

Mona recovered in time to mount up and ride—faster than usual when they looked back, atop a rise, to see a dotted line of camp fires off to the northeast. For it was an army column, sure as shooting, and they didn't want to be anywhere near once the shooting commenced.

Figuring both sides would be busy for a spell, Longarm threw caution to the winds and led them along a wagon trace that night, making far better time till the false dawn to the east warned them they'd best start scouting for another day camp.

But the range all about rolled grassy, as if someone had been at the chaparral with machetes and fall burn-offs. Mona said someone had, once they'd come to a fork in the trail where someone had put up a crude shrine.

When she asked Longarm for some light and he struck a match, muttering about the damned flame being visible a good three miles, the local gal clapped her hands and said she'd thought that was where they might be.

The carved wooden Cristo on the old rugged cross had looked a bit more like an Aztec sacrifice to Longarm. But Mona insisted there was a Christian pueblo, a friendly one, less than two hours away. So they rode, and she was wrong. It only took them an hour and a half to get there, just about at cock's crow. Folks rode faster at night when they were expecting to get shot at.

There was always somebody awake in a Mex pueblo. So they'd no sooner reined in out front of the posada Mona directed them to when the old gray alcalde and a delegation of village elders came on foot across the dusty plaza, hat in hand, to ask La Señorita what in the name of the Mother of God she was doing there.

It made more sense once Mona had evoked the name of her father and the alcalde had mentioned that gringo warrant he'd received by post rider. Alcalde was often translated as mayor, and an alcalde did that too. But he was as much the local justice of the peace, in charge of upholding such law as he felt able. So he told Mona, "First we had better get La Señorita and her friends out of sight. A rurale patrol passed through here less than a week ago. Meanwhile, I shall send a rider, poco tiempo, for to tell our patron, El Don Eduardo, his daughter has returned from the land of Los Gringos Rudo alive and well. I am sure they have already planned for how they can hide you until the right authorities can be bought off."

Longarm was sure too. So, since it was getting brighter by the minute, he agreed they should all get inside the posada for the day. He told Mona not to talk dumb when she whispered she wanted to be in the same room with him. A Mex posada charged far less than even a humble wayside inn up north. So he was able to hire a corner room with cross ventilation for just himself.

Mona said she was glad, when they were going at it dog-style later. It was hotter than the hinges of hell out in the hallway she'd just crept down. But naked flesh cooled good sweating in a really dry breeze.

Longarm had ridden this way before, so he knew, better than Mona, why she seemed so frantic to have him come in her, over and over, all that morning. When she finally had mercy on him, along about eleven, she softly pleaded, "How long do you think you may remember my sweet flowers, alma de mi corazón?"

He vowed he'd never forget them, and he meant it. For you never really forgot the really swell ones, and land's sake, hadn't that pretty little Tennessee gal asked the very same thing, long ago and maybe a day's march from Shiloh?

Her name had been . . . Billie? Either way, her freckled flesh had smelled of new-mown hay and their pubic bones had rubbed together so hard with the firm soil under her young behind in that shady old orchard and she'd said . . .

Said what, and where was he right now, he wondered in the few moments it took a man to realize he'd dozed off and then woken up all the way.

Once he had, he could see by the slant of the sunbeams coming through the jalousie slats from outside that he'd been asleep a good while. So that made him anxious enough to check all his fool belongings and bar the damned door the fool gal had left unlocked as she'd slipped out to the crapper, her own room to get dressed, or wherever.

The watch at one end of the chain it shared with his pocket derringer said it was after three. He whistled, rose, and moved to the window for a look-see. The plaza out front was deserted.

He wasn't surprised. It was siesta time. Late siesta time. The pueblo would be coming back to life pretty soon.

Meanwhile, Mona's dear old dad and his vaqueros figured to show up any time now. Longarm didn't feel like meeting anyone in his birthday suit. So he washed off at a corner stand and took his time getting dressed. He was glad he'd slept through La Siesta. It was almost impossible to be served down this way between noon and late afternoon, and he was hungry as a wolf in winter after all that healthy exercise followed by a good long nap.

His watch assured him La Siesta should be over by the time he had his hat on straight and tried one last time at the window. But the plaza was still deserted and it was quiet as a graveyard out yonder.

He doubted anyone had heard him and Mona going at it earlier through such thick 'dobe walls. Mex folks knew how to really enjoy an otherwise tedious time of day. Folks were likely coming bare-ass all over town. But meanwhile, damn it, he was hungry, and a cool drink wouldn't kill him either.

He moved out into the hall. It would have been darker and even stuffier had not some other doors been open. As he passed the room he suspected Concho and Lucia had been sharing, he glanced in to see a teenaged chica cleaning up in there instead.

When he asked, the young Mestiza told him, in a small scared voice, that El Don Eduardo had sent for his daughter a good three hours before, and that La Señorita Desdemona and her Lucia were on their way to who knows where.

When he asked if she'd seen Concho Morales, she said she thought he might be downstairs in the cantina. So that saved him asking if anything was open in town yet. The poor little gal sure seemed to be scared of gringos. They likely didn't see many in these parts.

He strode on to the stairwell and went down to the sort of dog run serving as their lobby. He spied old Concho through the archway to his left. The young Mex was seated at a small table painted the bright shade of blue they thought scared flies away down here.

When Concho waved wearily back, as if he'd had a rough morning, Longarm surmised he'd had to part with old Lucia the hard way.

For such a romantic-natured little thing, Mona had been more practical about sailing on without last-minute weeping and wailing. Or maybe she hadn't wanted to introduce him to her dear old daddy. But either way, Concho would have had to be there to be paid for *other* services rendered.

As he stepped through the archway Longarm asked Concho whether he gotten the money promised him. Concho's mouth smiled, but his eyes never did, as he replied in Spanish, "Not as much as I still have coming to me, Brazo Largo!"

Longarm tried. But before he could get to his gun he was jumped from either side of the archway. Before he could shake off either cuss holding each of his arms someone else shoved a mighty stiff dick, or a gun barrel, in the small of his back, while hissing, "Please make one move, you sucker of your father's cock. I have not been allowed for to shoot a gringo cocksucker for days!"

So Longarm just stood still as yet another gray-uniformed rurale with a big sombrero and crossed ammunition bandoleers took his own six-gun and, unhooking the handcuffs from the back of Longarm's gun rick, purred, "Hey, these are nice strong-looking manillas. Where is the key?"

Longarm shrugged, as much as he was able, and replied, "Saddlebags, upstairs. They ain't locked all the way, so—"

Then the sons of bitched had his wrists together behind him, and as the cold steel closed around them with a mighty determined click the rurale said, "They are *now*. Be good and maybe we shall take them off before our capitán directs us for to shoot you or for to hang you, eh?"

Longarm sighed and said, "You'd best consider holding us for trial, it being an election year, with me having at least a few Mex friends in high places. I ain't done anything down this way recently, and as for Señor Morales there . . ."

142

Concho laughed and said, "Don't worry about *me*, ass-hole." Then he nodded at the rurale who'd just cuffed Longarm, warning, "He's got a derringer at one end of that innocent-looking watch chain, Sargento."

As the rurale in command helped himself to the watch as well, Longarm nodded murderously at Concho and quietly asked, "What was the best offer, thirty pieces of silver?"

Concho chuckled fondly and replied, "You were worth more than that to the state of Chihuahua alone. As you just said, this is an election year and the peones in these parts will be pleased to see the murderer of their own Pepillo Zapatero brought to justice."

Longarm started to ask a dumb question. Then he recalled Mona's old manservant dropping out of sight up in Chrysolite. Old Mona had been surprised he'd never come back after sulking off that way.

Scowling at Concho, Longarm demanded, "How in thunder did these boys find out what you did to that poor old cuss this soon?"

Concho said, "*I* was not the one who knifed him so I would not have him getting between me and a stupid but not bad-looking mujer. I naturally told the authorities down this way you had murdered a Mexican citizen, while I was wiring them I was enticing you south so these rurales could assist me in your capture."

The rurale sergeant said, "I am sure all of this would be most interesting if I knew what you two were talking about or gave a mierdita. Pero now we had all better ride for that much bigger army column to our north. For they say both the Yaqui and Apache have been raiding in force and I do not wish for to be caught out after dark by either!"

Concho rose, saying, "Our own mounts are out back with your own, Sargento. His saddle and other valuables are up in his room. Shall I get them?"

The gruff rurale sergeant smiled thinly and said, "No. I would rather have one of my muchachos go through those saddlebags this one just mentioned. I may seem a simple soul to you, but I think I see what he meant about thirty pieces of silver."

The sergeant nodded at one of the rurales holding Longarm. As the Mex let go and turned to go upstairs Concho grinned sheepishly and asked, "Mierda, do you think I would be stupid enough to betray *you,* Sargento?"

The burly rurale smiled right back and said, "Since I'll never give you the chance, we'll really never know, will we?"

"They don't trust me," Concho pouted mockingly at Longarm.

The trail companion he'd just played false started to say he could prove he'd never had the chance to kill old Pepillo Zapatero that night in Chrysolite. He never did, because there was just no way he could evoke Mona and her maidservant as witnesses without getting a real pal in a whole lot of trouble.

Nodding at the treacherous Concho, he said, "They'd as likely find other charges if I was able to prove it was you who murdered that poor old cuss. But just to satisfy my curious nature, how in blue blazes did you manage to wire anyone that night after that Shadowy Saunders ordered the only wire cut?"

Concho shrugged and replied in an uncaring tone, "I never heard of those road agents before you rode in that night. Nobody cut our line to Shakespeare. Guess who that hard-drinking Pink Atwell left in charge of the company telegraph."

Longarm whistled and replied in mock admiration, "I'd guess old Shadowy Saunders can't hold a candle to you as an all-fired sneak. But if you wasn't in on anything with them other sneaks, how come you wanted to keep everyone in Chrysolite out of touch with the outside world?"

Concho shot a thoughtful glance at the rurales. But as Longarm had hoped, a bragging sneak found it hard to resist such a chance to show off to a professional sneak-catcher. So he smugly confided, "I didn't want to keep everyone out of touch. Just old Pink, once I'd decoded a wire intended for him. Seems Tucson suspected a party wanted on a California murder warrant might be headed for Mexico by way of our remote border crossing. When I noticed how close Tucson's description matched some folks who'd just blown into town—"

"I get the picture." Longarm said before the braggart could paint a clearer one for a rurale sergeant who spoke a fair amount of English.

To keep Concho from really screwing up, Longarm said, "You were doubtless trying to make up your mind which way you'd make the most money when I blew into town and . . . Hold on, you said at that time I had no way to prove who I was by wire."

"It was my boss who thought the telegraph was not working," the grinning sneak said. "He was sincere. I'd just disconnected one little wire, behind the battery jars. After he wandered off to bed with his bottle I naturally indulged my own curiosity. Denver sure speaks highly of you. Did you think I'd risk my pretty neck in Yaqui country for a lousy five hundred, even with another good gunhand backing my play, if I hadn't known you were the real El Brazo Largo, worth twice that much, *before* I wired you'd killed yet another Mexican citizen in cold blood, you cold-blooded hijo de puta."

"Manjate. You're not man enough to screw your *mother*!" Longarm replied in kind. Then the rurale returned with his saddle, saying, "He's got no dinero, no tobacco, but some nice gringo soap here in these saddlebags, Sargento. I did not see that key he mentioned."

Longarm protested, "It's *got* to be there, in the left bag. How am I ever going to get out of these handcuffs without the key?"

The sergeant chuckled and said, "Perhaps you were never meant to. Outside. I want to join up with those federales before sundown."

As they marched him out the back way Longarm protested, "Condenado, no me quibres culo. I can't ride with my hands cuffed behind me like this!"

The sergeant said, "You had better be able to. We shall shoot you without stopping if you fall off out in Yaqui country."

Chapter 16

Longarm wasn't worried about falling off as he loped through the chaparral that afternoon with his hands cuffed behind him while the treacherous Concho led his army gelding. The rurale sergeant and his eight-man squad were what he was worried about. They'd have doubtless found his backup derringer, pocket knife, and such without Concho's helpful hints. But he'd fibbed a bit about that handcuff key in his saddlebag. As long as he kept pleading with them to look again, they might not wonder why any professional with a set of cuffs clipped to his gun rig would leave the fool key in such a fool place. Like his tweed suit pants, the jeans he had on at the moment came with a small extra pocket, high up and sort of hidden by the empty gun rig he still had on. The pocket was a bit too small and unhandy for the small change some packed that way. But Longarm had found it a swell place to stow his handcuff key. So the question before the house was when and where he wanted to risk it.

He knew he'd only have the one chance. Rurales tended to be quick on the trigger even when they weren't all that pissed at anyone. They'd doubtless jump at the chance to gun a gringo out of hand and save themselves the tedium of hauling him all the way home. But if risking their anger out on the range was a good way to die young, waiting till they had him against a wall or under a gallows tree sounded worse. So he was figuring on that tricky light just after sundown, when everything was that same blurry brown and you had to be really good to hit a moving target.

Unfortunately, despite what some Texas riders were inclined to say, Los Rurales were good. El Presidente Diaz depended more on his rough-riding rural rangers to hold down the lid on a seething population of pissed-off peones. So he spared no expense when it came to arming and training his gray-clad pets, and rurales got far more target practice with their Yanqui Colt .45s than your average U.S. Army trooper.

Hoping sundown would catch them out on this rolling rough grazing before they joined up with those damned federales, Longarm enticed more brags out of Concho, seeing as they had to ride together in any damned case.

Longarm wasn't surprised to hear Concho brag that even though he'd kept things to himself, once he'd verified a strange rider's identity, old Pink Atwell would never say shit about tossing anyone down any mine shaft. Concho had simply made that up lest Longarm turn down his kind offer to escort two good-looking women home by way of Yaqui country.

Longarm knew that by now that rider they'd sent in to Shakespeare would have had time to send dozens of wires back and forth about a poor soul who'd been on the same side all the while. So that meant he only had to get away from these asshole rurales, and then make it back through all those asshole Yaqui, with no help, in time to set things up right in Chrysolite.

Knowing their telegraph really worked, and that their company police were harmless assholes, was likely to help a lot. But he had no way to wire for backup right at the damned moment, and scan the low chaparral all around as he might, he couldn't spy a damned bit of cover a man could use just long enough to get out of those damned cuffs and make a break for.

That was simply because he didn't know the foothills of the Sierra Madre as well as most Yaqui, or even most Mexicans.

For a rurale yelled, "Ay, Dios mio! Los Indios! De la izquierda!" just before a not-too-distant rifle squibbed to blow him off the right side of his rearing pony!

It wasn't easy, dismounting from the wrong side at a lope with one's hands cuffed behind one's back, but Longarm did it, having been informed by both that rurale and the shot that killed him that the Indians were over to the west.

He landed ungracefully, but still alive, on his left hip and shoulder in a cloud of dust. He'd rolled behind some other brush before anyone thought to spang a rifle round through that dust cloud, if anyone did. He saw Concho and another rurale getting blown out of their saddles. Then he was more busy with his own problems to pay all that much attention.

Lying on his side, Longarm pulled up his legs so he could loop his rump over his cuffed wrists. Once he had his hands cuffed in front of him it was simple to unlock the cuffs with the key he'd had all this time in his jeans.

Free at last, but dismounted and disarmed in the middle of a mighty confusing ambush, Longarm commenced to advance on the sound of the guns. It sounded stupid as hell. That was why armies trained their recruits to do so. Old soldiers never died because old soldiers didn't make the instinctive moves of new recruits, or natural human beings. Military field tactics were based on what a natural human being might do, by instinct. So as Longarm slithered through the greasewood toward all those damned guns going off, with no gun to call his own, a poor old rurale who'd naturally been slithering the other way, away from the sound of the guns, let out an awful wail that he'd been taken alive by Yaqui.

Longarm met up with old Concho, who hadn't been yet. His erstwhile trail companion was hit bad, high and low, but he was still alive. So Longarm whispered, "Howdy, Concho. Where in the hell is your gun? I could sure use one better than *you're* in shape to, old son."

Concho croaked, "That pendejo who was going through your own saddlebags just went through all my pockets. So he's got all our money too! Kill the cocksucker for me when you catch up with him, Longarm!"

Longarm didn't waste time answering. As he crawled on, Concho called after him, "Wait, don't leave me like this for the Yaqui *alive*! Come back here and kill me quick, you bastard!"

Longarm kept going, muttering, "Takes one to know one, I reckon."

He didn't have the thinking to spare about the wounded man's final fate. As he slithered on that other old boy they'd taken alive in the distance let out a girlish scream as they must have done something mighty mean to him. What any Indian was apt to do to a captured enemy was not a cheerful subject to dwell on. He felt a lot better when he met a totally dead rurale behind some blood-spattered bluebonnets. He helped himself to the dead man's whole gun rig as well as his Colt M-73 with a full seven inches of barrel throwing .45-50 longs. Los Rurales didn't worry about a kick your average cowhand would flinch at. They packed serious guns for serious shooting.

Suddenly the Yaqui shot seriously through those knee-high bluebonnets, but only hit the dead rurale again. Longarm put some distance between himself and a known target, risking a peek now and again for something to shoot back at.

He failed to see anything. Yaqui were good at not being seen, and worse yet, spattered him with greasewood flowers and cactus pulp every time he tried. So after he'd had his hat blown off a time or two, he just slithered on low till he found himself slithering over the rim of a shallow wash.

Shallow was still better than being pinned down in sticker bush that couldn't stop bullets for shit. So that was doubtless why he found himself with that rurale sergeant and three of his remaining men in the sandy eight-foot-wide and two-foot-deep depression. As their eyes met, the sergeant hissed, "This is no time for cristianos to quarrel among themselves. Agreed, El Brazo Largo?"

Longarm said, "I'm hoping you know how to fight good too. What happens once we fight our way out of this fix, Sargento?"

The burly Mex laughed dryly and replied, "Mierda, what is there about the way you are raised in El Norte? You are all such eternal optimists! Who said anything about fighting our way out? They have us by our cojones, and there is nothing left for us but to make the cochinos work at it and maybe take one or two with us, eh?"

Longarm kept the muzzle of his salvaged .45 trained neither too rudely nor too stupidly. "That's not what I asked," he said. "Why should I lift a finger to help four rascals who've been saying all day they meant to watch me die?"

The sergeant smiled crookedly and shot back, "We are all going to die, one way or another. Would you really rather die with the assistance of a Yaqui skinning you alive?"

Longarm said, "I don't aim to let them take me alive, and that goes double for you gents now that you've lost the edge on me."

The sergeant smiled wickedly and exclaimed, "Que pendejo! What do you think you could do with one six-shooter against the four of us, El Brazo Largo?"

To which Longarm could only modestly reply, "Shoot four times and have two rounds left. I reloaded the one empty chamber the cuss I took it off felt more comfortable with."

Before the sergeant could answer they heard a distant wail of hysterical agony. It sure sounded as if they might be skinning a castrated choirboy alive. Longarm warned, "They're just trying to spook us from this tolerable position."

The somewhat older rurale sergeant snorted in disgust and suggested the turisto penejo teach him how to make tortillas. Then he called up the draw, "Hunfredo, watch the chaparral to your right. If they are ready for to move in, they will be moving in from the west."

Hunfredo fired, ducked in time to only catch one round with the high crown of his gray felt sombrero, then popped up a another two yards away to observe. "Not anymore. If I did not *get* the culebra, I most certainly sent him slithering back to his mamita!"

The sergeant glanced skyward, observing, "They can see

that maldito sun as well as we can. They know we have less than four hours of daylight left. So they can afford to wait. But we had better be on guard for another try before dark. If anyone with a human brain could predict what might be going on in a Yaqui's head, we'd have rounded the wild beasts up by this time, eh?"

That one old boy they'd captured screamed again, mercifully a bit weaker. Longarm observed, "He's likely bled too much to feel what they're doing to him as much."

The sergeant nodded soberly and said, "I intend to save more than one last round for myself. One's hand is inclined to shake when one is terrified. My common sense tells me it would be best for to simply shoot myself at sundown, while I still have a clear choice. But ay, que frivolo, I shall probably try to stay alive a few more momentos, only to wish in the end I had not."

Longarm smiled thinly and said, "I know the feeling. I think it was that crusty old Duke of Wellington who said the art of winning was to last as long as you possibly could, and then last just five minutes longer. You see, it looked as if old Napoleon the First had the Iron Duke betwixt a rock and a hard place at Waterloo, till late in the fight when these reinforcements who'd got lost stumbled out of some woods into old Napoleon's flank and . . ."

"Madre de Dios, don't you ever give up?" the burly rurale said. "That federale column I was hoping to join forces with by sundown had to be a good twenty kilometras away when these Yaqui opened up on us. If there were any federales any closer these Yaqui would not have opened up on us, cabrón optimisto!"

Longarm didn't answer. It hurt worse to mention water when you just didn't have any. So he asked if he might have one of his own damned cheroots back.

The sergeant laughed harshly and said, "The hombre who went through your saddlebags is the one we hear screaming from time to time."

Longarm frowned thoughtfully and said, "They've had time

to get all that silver dinero old Concho must have had some-where on him too. He told me one of your boys robbed him. He'd have said so if it had been you, Sargento."

The boss rurale shrugged and said, "In that case the Yaqui have it by now. None of us here took time to rob the dead and wounded. I think that is for why we made it here. Does it really matter who has the dinero of that treacherous lambioso?"

Longarm said, "Sure it does. Indians have to pay for luxuries such as calico, salt, and bullets same as anyone else. That bounty Concho started out with this afternoon would pay for a mighty fine Yaqui hoedown. So maybe they're feeling too cheerful right now to risky dying at the end of a battle they can already brag on winning."

The older Mex grimaced and said, "Yaqui are never cheer-ful. I fear they are simply conserving their ammunition out there as they wait for it to get dark."

Longarm had no answer for that. So he just tried to settle a bit more comfortably on the sunbaked sand as it got still as an open grave for a spell. That screaming captive had either died or been carried off for more delicate surgery out of earshot. Critters didn't have much to say on such arid range in late afternoon. But the rurale up the wash called Hunfredo wasn't content to let the sun go down so quietly. He kept saying the Yaqui had gone home for to fuck their mamitas while he was dying for a smoke. Longarm didn't think the cucas he'd had in his saddlebags had been rolled with plain old tobacco. But he wasn't sure the poor simp was a serious addict until Hunfredo got to his feet and pegged a round at nothing in particular, demanding, "Pues . . . Are you still there?"

They were. Hunfredo was hit at least half a dozen times as he dropped out from under his big hat to sprawl limp and lifeless as a wet dishrag on the dry burning sand.

It got quiet again. The sergeant swallowed spit and softly said, "Maybe he knew what he was doing. He'll never feel it now when they slice off his agentes and shove them in his dead mouth."

Longarm didn't have an answer for that either. It was surprising how fast that old sun could streak across a cloudless sky when you wanted it to stay up there a spell.

It seemed like less than five minutes later, although it was likely a good two hours, when the sergeant broke the silence by croaking, "Is no use for to pray when you know nobody is listening. For as El Presidente has often remarked, we are so close to Los Yanquis and so far from any god! No matter what we do, they are going to cut off our noses, gouge out our eyes, shove our pitons down our throats, and—"

"Stuff a sock in it and die like a man," Longarm said suddenly. "I know there's no dignity later, once we're all bloated and flyblown. But that's just spoiled meat. You can't call a dead man a sissy no matter *what* anyone may do to him once he has no *say* in the matter. But if your manhood means toad squat to you, don't you go to weeping and wailing while you still draw *breath,* hear?"

The boss rurale was annoyed enough to stop praying and declare he was sure El Brazo Largo would shit his pants, the same as the rest of them, once the Yaqui moved in after sundown.

Longarm said he didn't see how either of them would collect on such a fool bet. That son-of-a-bitching sun was sinking so fast it reminded him of the second hand on a hangman's clock. The shadows were already so long there was no direct sunlight to light up the flat sands of their shallow wash. They didn't enjoy the shade as much as they might have otherwise.

One of the other rurales had removed his hat to pray on his knees, just their side of the dead Hunfredo. But the sergeant had recovered enough to hang tough, or pray silent, as he stared off to the west at that sinking sun.

Longarm figured they'd hear the rascals firing before they saw or heard anything else. But he was mighty surprised when they did hear a rapid-fire fusillade off to their north. For it sounded at least a quarter mile or more away.

Longarm sighed and said, "There you go, Sargento. Them federales must have heard our own gunplay down this way, and the Yaqui saw them coming before we could."

The boss rurale scowled and said, "I don't see how they could have ridden so far so soon." Then he brightened and rose to his feet, shouting, "Y qué, as long as they *did* it! Caramba! I see a battle flag and gunsmoke, a stupendous amount of gunsmoke, and look at those Indians *ride!*"

Longarm rose just high enough to verify a whole lot of dust as a whole lot of somebody tore off toward the higher sierras and the gunshots seemed to get more scattered.

The boss rurale fired his own gun thrice, and jumped up out of the wash to wave his big hat until, sure enough, a red and white guidon, followed by a mounted skirmish line, materialized from all that dust and smoke to head their way.

The rurale sergeant turned with a surprisingly pleasant smile to tell Longarm, "I shall mention your reasonable behavior to my superiors, pero now, if you would be good enough to drop that .45, El Brazo Largo . . ."

Longarm shook his head and said, "I'd as soon hang on to this until I've time to go gather up my own stuff where I hope it may still lie scattered back there. I don't want to use it on any of you gents after all we've been through. So don't make me."

The boss rurale blinked and said, "Ay, que nalgasón, you dare to threaten us, standing there with one pendejo pistol, as a whole column of Mexican cavalry bears down on you?"

Longarm shook his head and replied, "That would be an asshole way to act. But look again, speaking of assholes."

The sergeant did, blanched, and made the sign of the cross as the young officer in the lead, dressed in mighty dusty U.S. Army blue, reined in to call out, "Never chase fleeing Apache into a sunset. Longarm, is that you? What are *you* up to down here?"

It was that young Second Lieutenant Thornbury and his whole platoon from the Fourth Cav.

Longarm called back, "Howdy, Lieutenant. That wasn't Apache you and your boys just sent packing. They were Yaqui, so that ought to settle the question whether colored recruits can fight Indians or not. Indians just don't come no more Indian than the Yaqui manage."

Young Thornbury gulped and declared, "Let's just agree my men and I made contact with some of Victorio's outriders. That's what the colonel just sent us over this way to do. We're all down this way cooperating with the Mexican army for a change. Weren't you about to tell us what in blue blazes you were doing this far south of the border?"

Longarm shot a thoughtful glance at the surviving rurales, who all smiled back at him, innocent as hell. So he nodded and decided. "Hunting outlaws with these Mex pals of mine. You're not going to want to ride all strung out after dark in these parts, Lieutenant. So what say you dig in right here for the night and I'll have a lot of time to tell you a mighty tangled tale."

Chapter 17

Nobody could tell Longarm where those rurales had gone by the time Thornbury's troop, patrolling in strength, rejoined its squadron better than forty-eight hours later. So this seemed a poor time to desert the U.S. Army, even though he hadn't officially joined it.

Uncle Sam's military expedition into Chihuahua was an ad hoc brigade made up of garrison reserves from as far west as the Arizona Territory and as far east as Arkansas and East Texas. So greenhorns and old Indian fighters, black, white, and Pawnee scout, worked with a mess of good, bad, trained, and untrained Mexicans to run Victorio to ground as the spring flowers faded, each day dawned hotter, and a civilian lawman who'd been sent down this way after someone else entirely fretted and waited for a chance to make a run for it.

The Indians seemed even more upset by the unusual situation. Old Victorio and his Nadéne quit raiding and concentrated more on trying to become invisible. The Yaqui retreated into the deeper canyons of the Sierra Madre and just sort of held their fire till the blue-clad saltu from the north suffered heat stroke or whatever.

But this time both governments had agreed they wanted their so-called Apache Problem solved for good, and there was no arguing Phil Sheridan had included Apaches in his notorious observation about the only good Indians. So they told Longarm they meant to end the bloody career of Victorio, at least, if it took all summer.

But fortunately they'd started sending back their sick or wounded, well escorted by dragoons, before Longarm could get shot up or arrested by anyone Billy Vail had never sent him to fight.

There were always more sick than wounded riding in the covered ambulance wagons. So, not having to worry too much about bumps as they worried a heap about Indians out on all those shimmering flats, they made damned good time up to Fort Bliss.

Longarm dropped out at El Paso, leaving the one army mount left in the care of a friendly dragoon as he explained he had to catch a train. For he'd run into the El Paso Western Union after loping on ahead, only to find, as he'd feared, that he'd wasted far too much time in Old Mexico and that the Scarecrow Gang had struck, as expected, near the end of the month, a good three days before.

Vail wasn't sore at Longarm for not being in Chrysolite when the road agents grabbed a payroll. He was sore at him because he'd been lollygagging so far off when the sons of bitches had stopped the *Overland* stage, not the *Butterfield* stage, just outside Denver in broad-ass daylight.

Longarm caught the D&RG north without taking any more time with wires that made you wait around if you wanted answers. So he did a heap of guessing as he spent the next fifteen hours on a creeping and crawling passenger train. It was easy to guess Gargoyle Gibson, an established liar, had deliberately sent him on a wild-goose chase. His outraged boss and the even sterner Judge Dickerson had agreed one good turn deserved another. So they'd picked up Splitlip Sally at the quarters he'd hired her, over the Chinese laundry, to languish in the female wing at the federal house of detention till she or her even uglier husband made more sense.

It was doubtless unconstitutional. But old Judge Dickerson held, and Longarm sort of agreed, a deal was only a deal when nobody dealt from the bottom. And saying a gang was fixing to stop a stage in New Mexico when they were planning on stopping one in Colorado could hardly be considered dealing from the top.

The fifteen-hour haul up to Denver would have hurt worse if he hadn't found a gal to flirt with in the club car. She was a widow woman who'd never been all that much when she'd been younger, and right now had to be a good ten years older than him. She had hair that reminded a man of dust and eyes the exact color of raw oysters. What he could see of her figure under her respectable but loose-fitting black dress left a lot to be desired. But she had a sweet smile and, once she got over her surprise when he offered her some peanuts and a refill for her schooner of sarsaparilla, a tart sense of humor and a good head on skinny shoulders.

She dimpled—he was surprised she could—and allowed she had nothing to read either. But conversation, and only conversation, was all he was going to get if they rode this train all the way to the North Pole, she informed him.

He said he was only going as far as Denver and wouldn't have started up with her if he hadn't seen she was a respectable lady a young country boy might be safe with.

So once she stopped laughing she said he could call her Miss Ellen, and proceeded to tell him more about a mighty ordinary life than he'd have cared to hear if he'd had a copy of the *Denver Post* handy. He said he was mighty sorry about her late husband dying of apoplexy in his hardware store like that, but had to admire any man who'd leave his woman so well off with insurance money and a going business.

As he'd hoped, she was more interested in his business than her own. So they got to mull his wild-goose chase over, again and again, as the steel wheels rumbled under them for many a mile.

The skinny little drab enjoyed puzzles, and being a woman, sort of, she was far more interested in the grotesque relationship, as she put it, between a dirty old humpback and a simple young gal with a harelip.

159

By the time they'd had their noon dinner together in the dining car up ahead, they were comfortable enough with one another so he could intimate Splitlip Sally tended to be passed around among men who didn't want to kiss her on the lips. Miss Ellen wrinkled her own slightly more kissable lips and said, "You're probably right about her being simple as well as disfigured. Has it occurred to you her reasons for remaining in Denver might have had nothing to do with her lost cause of a husband?"

Longarm nodded. "Soon as I heard their gang stopped a stage that left from close to where she picked up needlessly high-priced delicatessen fare on a regular basis. She told me right out Shadowy Saunders enjoyed her dubious charms now and again. She said it had been just awful, against her will, but . . ."

"That's what we all say when we know we shouldn't enjoy it," Miss Ellen said with a roguish twinkle.

He twinkled back. "That's what I was about to assume. They got Gargoyle to throw us off the scent by sending me on a wild-goose chase. That gave 'em time to set up another hideout, doubtless right in Denver. They stopped that outward-bound stage, doubled back into town with the money, and even as we speak they're holed up as snug as bugs in that rug, waiting for things to cool down so they can simply leave by rail and start all over in other parts."

She demanded, "How did your fellow deputies know where to pick up that silly Splitlip Sally Gibson if the gang has a new hideout?"

He said, "I told them where I'd left the poor helpless waif as the country boy she played me for. From the few descriptions we have, Shadowy Saunders and the rest of the gang can get by out in public as ordinary-looking folk. They had the less ordinary-looking Gargoyle and his harelip off a ways with those Mexican riders, who'd raise eyebrows in your average Denver boardinghouse as well. So old Saunders likely told her to just stay put where a fool lawman like me put her while he, meanwhile, set up another hideout or more."

"Some sort of workplace where nobody would find Mexican workmen odd, coming or going?" she asked, brightly.

He nodded. "Along with an even more innocent-looking setup for himself and his current Anglo pets. He's ready to sacrifice or at least run out on any gang members who get picked up. Remind me to mention that to Splitlip Sally when we get into Denver this evening. I know why Gargoyle feels he ought to stay loyal. The two of 'em met up in Leavenworth. So there's no saying how many favors, or disfavors, a boss crook with plenty of money could do for an old pal in prison."

Miss Ellen made some other suggestions, maybe a third of them sensible, as they rumbled and rattled on till, in truth, he got so tired of talking in circles that he asked her to tell him more about her eight years of matrimony and six of widowhood. From her description of her recent visit to kin down El Paso way, widow women had to worry about men who seemed to hanker for a change from younger pretty gals. She said she'd never be able to look her niece in the eye again, and asked if Longarm thought it was her duty to write a letter about a wayward husband Longarm found downright stupid as well as mighty desperate.

He told Miss Ellen her niece doubtless knew. The wives of such compulsive idiots usually did, and she agreed that since nothing had really happened that *she* had any call to be ashamed of, she'd doubtless be better off letting somebody else clean the rascal's plow.

Later Miss Ellen began to doze, and Longarm began to do some serious thinking. Stopping trains instead of stages was the way most gangs favored since the Reno brothers had figured out how, right after the war. But a stage was still far easier to stop. It always would be, as long as stages still ran. But like the beaver trade, and even more recently the buffalo business, robbing stages for fun and profit would soon be a memory old farts just jawed about as they sat out on the steps of an evening, spitting and whittling.

So how much longer could Shadowy Saunders be planning to stay in business? That story Longarm had been sold about the Butterfield spur had sounded better in Judge Dickerson's chambers than down yonder where the fool line seemed to be dying by degrees.

The few stage lines that still ran any distances, with anything worth robbing aboard, tended to run west of the Great Divide, where the railroads were not as extensive. Gargoyle Gibson had met that ugly little wife of his in Utah too, come to study on it, shortly after getting out of prison. So how come they'd all come over here on the eastern slopes of the divide if Gargoyle had been scouting for . . . What? It couldn't have been a harelip with a nice ass who'd love him for his inner self.

Miss Ellen's mousy head was resting on his shoulder by the time the train rolled into the Union Yards in Denver. She seemed a bit confounded when he had to wake her. She got all red-faced when he confirmed she had indeed fallen asleep in the arms of a stranger, if you wanted to put it mighty silly. She seemed to feel somewhat calmer once he'd pointed out he'd only had that one arm around her shoulder to keep her from falling off the seat the other way, and that nobody you'd spent that much time with and told so many family secrets to could be considered a stranger in any case.

So she let him help her off with her carpetbag as he toted his far heavier load on the other hip and, outside the depot, she shyly gave him her business card, in case he ever wanted any hardware.

He didn't want anything she might have to offer, hard or soft. But he kissed the back of her hand anyway when she held it out to him. From the way she flustered he figured she'd only meant to shake hands, but it didn't seem to really make her mad. So they parted friendly, in that awkward way experienced travelers part company with new old friends they'll likely never see again.

Downtown Denver was almost totally shut down for the night, of course, but they never closed at the federal house of detention west of the federal building. So that's where he went once he'd checked his saddle and such in at the depot.

He'd pick them up on his way to his hired digs on the far side of Cherry Creek later on.

Aside from the usual uniformed turnkeys, he found Smiley and Dutch, from his own office, playing checkers but armed and dangerous near the booking desk downstairs. The shorter and more jolly-looking Dutch was the more dangerous of the two deputies. Smiley was the last name of a hawk-faced breed who never smiled, but had a much more predictable temper. Longarm howdied them and told the desk sergeant what he was doing there.

Dutch didn't get sore, but said, "You can't go up. Marshal Vail is holding both them Gibsons uncommunicated. That's what the two of us are doing here at this infernal hour, making sure they stay uncommunicated."

Longarm dryly replied, "I think you mean incommunicado, Dutch. I don't see how Billy Vail could mean me."

Dutch insisted, "I don't know, pard. There was this lawyer in here earlier, threatening to do wonders and eat cucumbers if we didn't let that harelip out at least on a written heap of corpses. He said we were heaping violets all over the constitution. Smiley wouldn't let me pistol-whup him, the silly son of a bitch."

Longarm smiled and said, "I hope you're calling the lawyer the son of a bitch. Old Billy may be violating the constitution if that writ of habeas corpus was any good. Did the lawyer have a name?"

Smiley said, "Newgate, Grover T. I never heard of him, and his writ was signed by some asshole on the state supreme court. When I told him he'd best go back for a federal writ before Dutch bit him on the leg, he said he'd be back with one."

Longarm sighed. "You should have let Dutch bite him on the leg. I know G. T. Newgate of old. He called me a liar in court one day. I keep expecting the bar association to rein him in, but so far he's managed not to bust through the thin ice he likes to skate on. I better go up and ask Gargoyle how he can afford such an expensive lawyer if his boss robbed him as he claims."

163

Dutch started to say something stupid about their orders. Smiley told him he was an asshole before Longarm had the chance.

The turnkey led him first to Gargoyle's cell in the men's wing. He wasted time and a perfectly good cheroot trying to get a grinning little shit to explain what was so funny about sending a lawman so far on a fool's errand. When Gargoyle launched into yet another self-serving tangle of excuses, Longarm got the turnkey to run him over to the woman's wing instead.

Splitlip Sally was locked up alone on Billy Vail's orders as well. The federal matron who'd gone back there with Longarm and the male turnkey to make sure they didn't gang-bang the prisoner said she was the one who'd told Marshal Vail the harelip had been receiving lots of visitors and more flowers, books, and candy than she, the matron, had seen in any one cell since she'd been hired to keep things right.

Longarm told the worried-looking harelip he was sorry all the flower stands had been shut by the time he got back, as she joined him at the bars with a shy, hideous smile.

Before she could wind up to feed him more bull he quickly added, "I know they've promised to get you out on a writ, Miss Sally. They might even *do* it, albeit Cockeyed Jack McCall had worse luck when his lawyer insisted they couldn't try a man twice for the same back-shooting. Let's talk about your true love, Shadowy Saunders, alias Hudson, alias Lord only knows, the shifty cuss."

She laughed incredulously, a frightening sight. Longarm nodded soberly and said, "You ain't that stupid. Nobody could be. Gargoyle is going away for a mighty long time, and anyone dumb enough to be waiting for him to get out would be better advised to wait a far piece off, especially now with this latest robbery you and the humpback were scouting for."

She swore she'd known nothing about any robberies before they'd taken place. So he said, "Spare me your swearing and let me try a way that works better. Your lover-boss and the other ordinary Anglo gang members could move, say, a

164

couple of streets over and be safe enough. There's a fair-sized Mex district over the other side of Cherry Creek, but our Denver Mexicans are inclined to gossip about newcomers to the neighborhood. So you all needed another place to hide those riders, preferably some distance from the Mex district, but somewhere their new Anglo neighbors would accept them as just a natural part of the scenery. So now I'd like you to tell me where Shadowy Saunders sent you to set up another business cover."

She stared through her bars like an innocent owl. So he nodded and tried, "That consumptive Canadian sneak may have you convinced he really liked you best all the time. But a lady I just met on a train makes me wonder. When I told her about your lip, no offense, she asked how come you couldn't get it fixed, seeing you had so many rich lovers. Any army surgeon who's ever doctored a tomahawk wound out to Camp Weld could likely fix you up easier, painless, since they've had chloroform and such to work with since before the war."

She sighed and said, "I mentioned that to my husband when we were first married. He said it was risky and that he liked me the way I was."

Longarm said, "I'll bet. We both know why a crippled runt might want to keep a fine-figured gal at his side most of the time. But why would your other rich lover want to leave you in such a fix if you mean anything at all to him? You say he's got a regular gal, Fat Alice, with a dumpy shape and a pretty face. Why would he leave a well-built gal like you so ugly if he cared a thing about you?"

She started to cry. He said, "I meant what I just said about a simple operation, at government expense, over at that near-by army surgery, Miss Sally. You don't even have to turn state's evidence. By now you've surely noticed my boss, Billy Vail, is inclined to bend a few rules in the interests of rough justice. Just put us on the trail of the the serious crooks we really want and you'll get to go pretty as well as free, hear?"

It didn't seem to be working. She started to hand him more bull about being no more than a simple country girl who'd been led astray by sweet-talking humpbacks and corn-holing consumptive Canadians. That reminded him of those wires he'd sent old Crown Sergeant Foster of the Northwest Mounted Police. So he warned Splitlip Sally she'd do well to get another lick of candy if she didn't wise up, and went next to the Western Union to see if the Mounties could suggest any better ways to identify their wayward lad on sight.

Next morning, bright and early, he met his stumpy boss, Marshal Vail, on the granite steps of the federal building. Billy Vail was so surprised to see Longarm report for work that early he forgot to frown as he asked, "Where in the hell have you been all this time?"

Longarm replied, "Never mind about me. Can we keep Splitlip Sally on ice at least until noon? I need time to paw through some local records at the county clerk's."

Vail said, "Hell, we can hold her till Judge Dickerson says we can't hold her, and that's likely to be some time. The boys already sent a message to my house on Capitol Hill about that law-slick and his asshole writ. I told them to tell him to wipe himself on it the next time he comes by. The literal meaning of habeas corpus is, 'Thou shalt have the body.' Meaning the accused has to appear in court or go free. It's only intended to keep a judge less slick than Judge Dickerson from holding someone indefinitely without good cause."

Longarm smiled thinly and said, "We ain't got good cause as the gal's been charged. A respectable Chinese pal of mind stands ready to back her story she was right upstairs, doubtless pacing the floor, with her husband in jail across town, when that Overland stage was stopped by persons so far unknown."

Vail snorted, "Shit, we know it was Shadowy Saunders. We just have to get her to tell us where the son of a bitch is!"

Longarm said, "She ain't going to. I want you and the boys to stall any attempts to get her out this side of lunch. I ought to be back before then, with some names and addresses. If you let her out this afternoon, so we can follow her, I'm sure we'll get at least one more."

He started to turn away. Vail scowled and said, "Hold on! Have you forgotten who's in charge of this infernal federal district? Where in blue blazes do you think you're going, to do what?"

Longarm reached in his frock coat for the night letter Crown Sergeant Foster had sent from Fort MacLeod days ago as he explained, "We know the name of their Denver lawyer. It's G. T. Newgate. Need I say more?"

Vail scanned the night letter from Canada as he muttered, "You do. Newgate is a shit-heel who'd sell out his mother, if it didn't put his own ass in a sling. But he'd be putting his ass in a sling indeed if he knowingly hid out a known outlaw gang!"

Longarm said, "I'm sure he knows better than that, Boss. But a gal who'd lie to a swell gent like me would be apt to lie to her own lawyer too."

Vail suddenly blinked down at the yellow paper in his fists, read over a passage again, and said, "That's for damned sure. Go get 'em, you human bloodhound!"

So Longarm did. It only took a few minutes at the files of the county clerk to find what he was looking for. Knowing the name of the attorney of record helped a heap. For as Longarm had hoped, the slick leader of the gang had made certain that the property the gang had bought or leased in advance was properly documented, lest anyone question someone's right to be on the premises doing anything they wanted. So a smart little file clerk who said she got off at six was able to dig out every real-estate closing G. T. Newgate Esquire had been involved in for a month of Sundays, just by cross-index.

Longarm didn't need them all. When the files showed Newgate had helped a client lease a furniture warehouse over by Platte, a few days after that fake cabinetmaking shop had been exposed, a mighty pleased federal deputy told the perky little brunette, "I see old G. T. handled the paperwork on that cabinetmaking shop to begin with. I was talking with someone else about clever criminals not long ago. Offhand, I'd say this bunch has been more devious than really smart."

Then he left, resisting the temptation to tell her what old Niccolò Machiavelli had said about being sneaky for the sake of being sneaky. Lots of assholes who'd never really read Machiavelli professed to admire him when they were acting contrary to what he'd really advised.

Longarm was still thinking about overly clever crooks when he got back to the office, to find Billy Vail had already called in deputies Gilfoyle, Kelly, Williams, and Feldman, all five of them armed to the teeth while young Henry just looked left out behind his typewriter.

Longarm held up the notepaper he'd brought back from the county clerk's, saying, "Same sort of setup, I'd say. Far enough from that cabinetmaking shop, yet a similar enough business in the unlikely event someone passing recognizes someone from the earlier place across town."

Vail grumbled, "Let's not worry about *why* they're hiding out in a fucking warehouse. Let's mount up and *ride* for that fucking warehouse!"

Longarm said it made more sense to walk. Billy agreed, by the time they got out front. For it was only half a mile to walk, and nobody had to hold any horses once they got there.

Better yet, when they did get there, the cavernous frame warehouse had its back wall, with only one exit on that side, to the open field of fire provided by the Denver stock and freight yards.

Billy Vail had recruited some Denver copper badges along the way. Denver P.D. hated to be left out, and always came running when they heard gunplay in any case.

But such gunplay as there was turned out sort of disappointing in the end. Only one excited Mexican tore out that back way, mounted on a paint pony, to get blown out of his saddle by Deputy Gilfoyle as he tried to make it through a stockyard gate at full gallop.

The rest surrendered within the hour, after lots of remarks about mothers, sex organs, and the possible use of coal-oil bombs on such an old dry building they'd been able to lease so cheap.

There were eight survivors in all. Three Anglo, five Mex, all of them male and inclined to mutter things like "Chingate!" when asked where their friends were.

Deputy Williams pistol-whipped one before Longarm could tell him not to, explaining, "We got others strings for our bow. Let's get these boys booked and locked away before lunch. I'm hoping a lady may lead us to the rest of her more respectable-looking pals this afternoon."

But she didn't. Longarm, Vail, and some other deputies watched from inside a shop across the way as Lawyer Newgate led his female client down the front steps of the house of detention in broad-ass daylight. Newgate seemed to want to take her somewhere, judging by his gestures from this distance. But Splitlip Sally seemed to have other plans. So after some jawing they shook and parted friendly.

Vail said, "She seems to be in a hurry," as the gal they were watching lit out at a brisk pace. So it was easy to follow her at a discreet distance catty-corner across the crowded street until, as Longarm had expected, she whipped into the Drover's Loans and Savings, a few blocks up from Union Depot.

Gilfoyle then said, "How's she going to rob a bank without a gun? They'd have never let her sneak a gun in or out of her old cell, would they?"

Longarm said, "She don't need a gun. She only needs a bankbook. She could have had that smuggled in to her easy amidst all them flowers, books, and candy."

Kelly frowned. "You mean she might have a regular bank account, like an honest gal?"

Longarm nodded. "She'd be dumb as hell to keep that much under any mattress. How did you think she meant to keep her followers from stealing it once she'd been picked up again?"

Gilfoyle was quick enough to say, "*Her* followers?"

Billy Vail was the one who explained. "Shadowy Saunders was a lie as well. I have met me some liars in this business, but I got to hand it to a gang of liars led by a dead man.

169

Fort MacLeod said Shadowy Saunders, alias James Hudson, died a year ago up their way, of the consumption everyone said was fatal."

Longarm said, "That's how I knew right off she was an even bigger liar than her so-called husband. He'd only told us a dead man he'd once served time with was their leader. She told me the the same dead man corn-holed her."

Kelly laughed and declared, "That sounds mighty desperate, even for a harelip!"

Longarm said, "No more than an ugly gal refusing a chance to be way better-looking. Free. Oops, here she comes back out. Let's see where she goes now, with all that money in that innocent old manila envelope."

It was easy enough to follow her and her bulky package. Old Vail figured it for as much as Overland had lost, converted to silver certificates of serious denominations, for after some awkward fooling with her hair she whipped into a fashionable dress shop on Seventeenth Street, a block west of the depot.

She took much longer in there than she had inside the bank. But once she came out, if that was really her, she'd really spent her time and a lot of money inside well. She was gussied head to toe in a big picture hat and a frilly summer dress of real lavender silk, and packing a big lady's handbag instead of that manila envelope.

Vail asked Longarm, "When do we move in on the literally two-faced bitch? How do you reckon she works that shit with the harelip?"

Longarm said, "Let's give her more rope. I suspect she got rid of that spring clip before she ducked into that fine lady's shop. Would you want to enter looking like a drab harelip and leave as a gussied-up beauty with no harelip at all?"

They had to move west after her in a hurry, as she sure did move those new lavender skirts. Gilfoyle half demanded and half sobbed, "What was that shit about a spring clip and looking like a harelip?"

"Stage-acting device," Longarm explained without breaking his long stride. When that failed to satisfy his fellow deputy

170

Longarm said, "There really was a Splitlip Sally riding as an outlaw up in Montana a spell back. Maybe there still is. But the late Shadowy Saunders never met up with *this* bunch, and what'll you bet Gargoyle Giboson ain't the real Gargoyle Gibson we got such good records on?"

Gilfoyle gasped, "Aw, shit, you can't fake a humpback like he has, damn it."

Longarm nodded. "You don't have to be the real Gibson to be born that way either, unfortunately. Don't you see it yet? That gal we're following—I'll bet you anything she's a failed or never-hired actress—put together this gang to pull off a quick bunch of robberies and then scatter to the four winds, as the real folks they started out, while you, me, and the rest of us assholes search high and low for better-known crooks that had nothing to do with any of their crimes."

"But we *have* a bunch of 'em now," Gilfoyle pointed out. "We only have to get one of them to talk and . . ."

"She knows that," Longarm said. "Why did you think she's been walking so fast? There's an eastbound express leaving within half an hour. So you boys better keep an eye on her while I cut left at the next alley and run like hell."

No federal lawman had to have that explained to him. So Longarm just lit out, then ran some more, a block over, to cross Wynkoop and reach another entrance to the depot before that lavender dress was in sight.

So he was standing in a shadowy niche near the newsstand when the innocent-looking beauty in lavender was greeted by a tall good-looking cuss in a seersucker suit, just inside the front entrance with two big leather grips. Longarm didn't move in as they kissed. He wasn't being sentimental. It was best to have a clearer field of fire before one moved in on a cuss who robbed folks at gunpoint for a living.

He let them move out to the platform. The eastbound express was just easing up the track. Longarm waited till the steel locomotive tender was creeping along on the far side of the couple before he took a deep breath, broke cover, and called out, "Freeze in the name of the law!"

The pretty gal he'd known as Splitlip Sally was smart enough to drop her handbag and reach for the sky. But her handsome escort went for the gun under his seersucker coat. So he naturally flew back against the moving tender with a round of .44-40 over his heart to bounce back and flop like a busted rag doll to the grimy cement platform between Longarm and the hem of those lavender skirts.

She kicked his limp form, hissing, "You stupid twit! How were they going to prove shit?"

He didn't answer. Longarm told her, not unkindly, "It's over, ma'am, whoever you are. I'll just leave the wrapping up to my sly old boss as I thank my stars I never took advantage of your kind offer that time."

As others gathered around she asked him brazenly, "Wouldn't you have screwed me had you known what I really looked like?"

He smiled sheepishly and replied, "I just said that. Fortunately, you never managed to compromise me as the arresting officer, and the more I study on it, the more tempting a certain little brunette or, hell, a good old gal with a hardware store seems to me right now!"

Watch for

LONGARM AND THE DIAMOND SNATCHERS

173rd in the bold LONGARM series from Jove

Coming in May!

The wolf loped through the brush, moving soundlessly over the sandy soil. From time to time it stopped, testing the air, scanning its surroundings, listening. It was an old wolf, had grown old because of its caution, because of listening, watching, never showing itself. There once had been many wolves in the area, but most were gone now, most dead, killed by men with rifles, and traps, and poison. This particular wolf had long ago learned to avoid man, or anything that smelled of man. And it had survived.

It was late spring; the sagebrush still showed some green. The wolf had been eating well lately, many animals browsed on that green, and the wolf browsed on the animals, the smaller ones, the ones he could catch by himself. There were no longer any wolf packs to pull down bigger game: deer, antelope. Life was now a succession of small meals, barely mouthfuls.

The wolf was thirsty. A quarter of a mile ahead a patch of thicker green showed. A water hole. The wolf could smell the water. It increased its pace, loping along, bouncing on still-springy legs, tongue lolling from its mouth, yellow eyes alert.

A thicket of willows some fifteen feet high, grew up on the far side of the water hole. The wolf gave them a cursory scan. It raised its nose, its main warning system, and could smell only water, willows, and mud.

It was late enough in the season for the water hole to have shrunk to a scummy puddle, no more than a foot deep and twenty feet across. In winter, when the rains came, the water formed a small lake. One more look around, then the wolf dropped its muzzle, pushed scum aside, and lapped slowly at the water. After half a minute the wolf raised its head again, turning it from side to side, nervous. The water had claimed its attention for a dangerously long time.

Suddenly, the wolf froze. Perhaps the horse had made a small movement. Horses do not like the company of wolves, yet this one had stood motionless while the wolf approached, held so by the man on its back. The wolf saw him then, the man, blending into the willow thicket, mounted, sitting perfectly motionless.

A moment's stab of fear, the wolf's muscles bunching, ready to propel him away. But the wolf did not run. Ears pricked high, it stood still, looking straight at the man, sensing that he meant him no harm. Sensing, in its wolf's brain, an affinity with this particular man.

Wolf and man continued to look at one another for perhaps a half a minute. Then the wolf, with great dignity, turned, and loped away. Within seconds it had vanished into the brush.

The man did not move until he could no longer see the wolf. Then, with gentle pressure from his knees, he urged the horse out of the willows, down toward the water hole, let it drink again. The horse had been drinking earlier, head down, legs splayed out, when the man had first seen the wolf, or rather, seen movement, about a quarter of a mile away, a flicker of grey gliding through the chaparral. He was not quite sure why he'd backed his horse into the willows, why he'd quieted the animal down as the wolf approached. Perhaps he wanted to see if it could be done, if he could become invisible to the wolf. Because if he could do that, he should be able to become invisible to anything.

The wind had been from the wolf's direction. The horse's hoofs had crushed some water plants at the edge of the pool; they gave off a strong odor, masking the man's scent, masking the horse's. A trick old Jedadiah had shown him, all those years ago . . . let nature herself conceal you.

He'd watched as the wolf approached the water hole, made one last cursory check of its surroundings, then began to drink. A big, gaunt old fellow. The man wondered how the hell it had survived. Damned stockmen had done their best to exterminate every wolf within five hundred miles. Exterminate everything except their cows.

He was aware of the moment the wolf sensed his presence, knew it would happen an instant before it actually did. He watched the wolf's head rise, its body tense. But he knew that it would not run. Or rather, sensed it. No, more than that . . . it was as if he and the wolf shared a single mind, were the same species. Brothers. The man smiled. Why not? Both he and the wolf shared a way of life . . . they were both the hunter and the hunted.

The wolf was gone now, the moment over, and the man, pulling his horse's head up from the water before it drank too much, left the pool and rode out into the brush. And as he rode, anyone able to watch from some celestial vantage point would have noticed that he travelled pretty much as the wolf had travelled, almost invisible in the brush, just flickers of movement as he guided his horse over a route that would expose him least, avoiding high ground, never riding close to clumps of brush that were too thick to see into, places that might conceal other men.

He rode until about an hour before dark, then he began to look for a place to make camp for the night. He found it a quarter of an hour later, a small depression surrounded by fairly thick chaparral, but not so thick that he could not see out through it.

Dismounting, he quickly stripped the gear from his horse, the bedroll and saddlebags coming off first, laid neatly together near the place where he knew he would build a small fire. He drew his two rifles, the big Sharps and the lighter Winchester, from their saddle scabbards, and propped them against a bush, within easy reach. The saddle came off next; he heard his horse

179

sigh with relief when he loosened the girth.

Reaching into his saddlebags, the man pulled out a hackamore made of soft, braided leather. Working with the ease
that comes from doing the same thing dozens of times, he
slipped the bit and bridle off his horse, and replaced it with
the hackamore. Now, the horse would be able to graze as
it wished, without a mouthful of iron bit in the way. More
importantly, if there was danger, if the man had to leave
immediately, he would have some kind of head stall already
on his horse. When trouble came, speed was essential, thus
the hackamore, and the style of his saddle, a center-fire rig,
less stable than a double rig, but easy to throw on a horse
when you were in a hurry.

The man fastened a long lead rope to the hackamore, tied
the free end to a stout bush, then left his horse free to move
where it wanted. He allowed himself a minute to sink down
onto the sandy ground, studying the area around him, alert,
but also aware of the peacefulness of the place. There was
no sound at all except the soft movement of the warm breeze
through the bushes, and, a hundred yards away, a single bird,
singing its heart out.

In the midst of this quiet the man was aware of the work-
ings of his mind. He was comfortable with his mind, liked
to let it roam free, liked to watch the way it worked. He
had learned over the years that most other men were uneasy
with their minds, tried to blot them out with liquor or reli-
gion.

His gaze wandered over to his horse. To the hackamore. He
remembered the original Spanish word for halter . . . *jaquima,*
altered now by the Anglo cowboy. Through his reading, and
he read a great deal, the man had discovered that many of the
words the Western horseman used were of Spanish origin, usually changed almost beyond recognition. When the first American cowboys came out West, they learned their trade from
the original Western settlers, the Spanish *vaqueros.* Matchless
horsemen, those Spaniards, especially out in California. God
they could ride!

180

When the Anglos moved into Texas, it was the local Mexicans who'd taught them how to handle cattle in those wide open spaces. Yet, he knew that most cowboys were totally unaware of the roots of the words they used every day. Not this man. He liked to think about words, about meanings, mysteries. He had an unquenchable hunger to learn.

And at the moment, a more basic hunger. There was movement off to his left; a jackrabbit, one of God's stupider creatures, was hopping toward him. The rabbit stopped about ten yards away, then stood up on its hind legs so that it could more easily study this strange-smelling object. Rabbit and man were both immobile for several seconds, watching one another, then the man moved, one smooth motion, the pistol on his hip now in his hand, the hammer snicking back, the roar of a shot racketing around the little depression.

Peering through a big cloud of white gunsmoke, the man thought at first he had missed; he could not see the rabbit. But then he did see it, or what was left of it, lying next to a bush a yard from where it had been sitting when he'd fired. He got up, went over to the dead rabbit. The big .45 caliber bullet had not left much of the head or front quarters, but that didn't matter. The hind quarters were where the meat was.

It took him less than five minutes to skin and gut the rabbit. He methodically picked out the big parasitic worms that lived beneath the rabbit's scruffy hide, careful not to smash them, and ruin the meat. Ugly things. It took another fifteen minutes to get a fire going, and while the fire burned down to hot coals, the man whittled a spit out of a springy manzanilla branch, and ran it through the rabbit.

It was dark before the rabbit was cooked. After seeing those worms, the man wanted to make sure the meat was done all the way through. He ate slowly, trying not to burn his fingers. For dessert he fished a small can of peaches out of his saddlebags. His only drink was warm, brackish water from his canteen. But he considered the meal a success, not so much because of the bill of fare, but because of the elegance of his surroundings: the pristine cleanness of the sandy ground on which he sat, the perfume of the chaparral, the broad band of the Milky Way arching overhead, undimmed.

Yeah, he thought, pretty damned beautiful. He scratched his chin through a week's unshaven bristle. And reflected that his life was damned lonely sometimes. Well, that was a choice he'd made, way back, and he was a man who stuck with his decisions.

Still, it could get damned lonely.

LONGARM

Explore the exciting Old West with
one of the men who made it wild!

419